Best regards
Marguerita Ogilvie

Crying on the Inside

White Wolf Woman

FriesenPress

Suite 300 - 990 Fort St
Victoria, BC, V8V 3K2
Canada

www.friesenpress.com

Copyright © 2021 by White Wolf Woman
First Edition — 2021

All rights reserved.

No part of this publication may be reproduced in any form, or by any means, electronic or mechanical, including photocopying, recording, or any information browsing, storage, or retrieval system, without permission in writing from FriesenPress.

ISBN
978-1-5255-8613-2 (Hardcover)
978-1-5255-8614-9 (Paperback)
978-1-5255-8615-6 (eBook)

1. Fiction, Family Life, Marriage & Divorce

Distributed to the trade
by The Ingram Book Company

[illegible manuscript]

The content of publication is based on actual events. Names have been changed to protect individual privacy. Opinions and theories are those of the author.

A Note from the Author

This novel will impact different people in different ways. If you've been the victim of spousal abuse, you'll immediately identify some of the patterns of abuse, and you might become aware of others. Some patterns will not even be mentioned. If you've never been a victim, you need to realize that abuse exists. It may be happening to your neighbour, your child, your grandchild, or even your mother. Chances are you know someone who is or has been a victim and you might not even recognize this or be aware of the many signs out there, as we don't always see them. Because of the feeling of shame our society still imposes upon victims, many will never admit to what is happening behind closed doors. Only the children will see, and they will think it's normal, as they know nothing else. But they will know when it's dangerous to stay home and will go to spend a night with friends. They learn to recognize honeymoon/egg-shell-walk/blow cycle and are very attune to when the blow is coming.

I once went arrowhead hunting. I knew where a friend of mine had found many arrowheads from past First Nations peoples, and I thought I wanted to find some too. I looked and looked for many days but didn't find a single one. I phoned my friend and asked him why I couldn't find them when he's found so many. He said, "You didn't know how to look or what you were looking for." This is so true about the signs of abusive relationships, but this book will make you aware of them. The signs are always there! To understand abuse, we need the knowledge, and this can be gained through experience, observation, and research. Then we too will be able to read the signs and make a difference.

> *Knowledge is power but only if we have it, and it's useless if we don't use it in an effective and meaningful way!*

At the time of this writing, I saw statistics that stated that 33 per cent of all women are abused by their spouses, and this is only what is known. There are many "silent" ones who aren't included as they keep it a deep secret and no one knows or will ever know. These victims learn to wear the "mask" and go unnoticed. Statistics are only as accurate as the facts allow them to be. I would venture to say that at least one in two is silent and not a statistic! Perhaps as a society we need to look at our methods of gathering statistics and how our legal system handles incidents of abuse. Not all abuse shows on the outside; there are many wounds and scars inside of us but they fall into patterns, that psychologists can readily identify. At the time of this writing, if there are no visible marks, no charges are laid; if no charges are laid, there are no statistics! These inner scars can lead to future illnesses, such as PTSD, fibromyalgia, and even cancer, as well as strokes or heart problems. The body can only take so much constant abuse, whether it is self-administered or inflicted by others. The mind controls the body, and when the mind is damaged, so too will the body be.

This is the first of a three part series of books, a trilogy on the topic of spousal abuse. The other two will follow in sequence and offer answers to questions posed in this book. Many men are abused by their spouses, as well, but the ratio of abused men to abused women is still 1:9 of "known" victims, which were statistics at the time of this writing. Even though many of the patterns are the same, there are some behavioral differences in how men deal with spousal abuse, because of our society's expectations of them.

> *In a sense, society dictates the characteristics of spousal abuse and the way it plays out.*

There will only be as much abuse as society will tolerate, and right now, it tolerates far too much. In the past, the United Nations chastised Canada for its acceptance of spousal abuse. We have become insensitive to what we hear on the news every day, and we deny that it could happen to one of us until we are impacted by something we never expected, or it's in our home, our town, our neighborhood! It can happen to anyone, and it's been recognized as happening to one out of three women in our society.[1]

I focus my books on the female victims of spousal abuse rather than try to cover all forms of spousal abuse in both genders. I also concentrated on psychological, emotional, and financial abuse, as these forms are too frequently accepted by our society. The victims of these types of abuse might be considered the "silent ones," as I have mentioned. I applaud the abuse laws dealing with psychological damage done to victims, as put through the UK parliament in early 2017. I also read with interest the working paper put out by the Saskatchewan government on psychological intimate partner abuse. I sincerely hope this province will put their findings into our criminal code and that Manitoba will follow suit. At the time of this writing it has not yet happened. Only when the justice system recognizes this abuse of victims, penalizes perpetrators, and mandates professional help for them will the incidents of spousal abuse against women decline. There is help for victims of physical and sexual abuse. There is compensation for victims of crime, but only if charges are laid. Victims as well as the abusers need professional counselling.

The forms of abuse I focus on are still grey areas, where only lip service is provided to curbing it. I have read literature on spousal abuse that indicated *"all abuse is considered a crime."* If this is the case, then why are so many emotional abusers out there abusing one vulnerable woman after another without being arrested? And why do we not mandate professional help for abusers as well as victims? Why are we not more proactive than reactive? Women still feel like they are subordinate to men, and they put up with more than they should. There are no ramifications for the perpetrators and no recourse for the victims, making our justice system a dismal failure for victims of these types of abuse. This needs to be addressed by our justice system as soon as possible. Our law makers also need to listen to the victims and encourage them to speak up, instead of muzzling them in the same way they muzzled me.

Men who need to control their partners, and do not wish to be arrested, will resort to verbal, emotional, and financial abuse instead, as they know they can get away with this. I once asked a man why he was abusing his wife,

---

1   Newspaper article of a murder or suicide in our home town

and he replied, "no one told me I couldn't do this!" In another instance, I asked a man why he was constantly cheating on his wife, and he also said it was because he could get away with it. Even if he were caught, his wife would still take him back.

In my own experience as a victim of abuse, I found a subtle prejudice against women who have been abused, throughout society. I say subtle because without seeking out answers, I would have never known this. Try getting financial help from a bank or any other lending agency when you're a victim. A victim of financial abuse likely won't have a good credit rating, but that doesn't mean she's irresponsible or doesn't pay her bills when she can. Credit reporting bureaus are merciless if a person is behind in paying bills, and financial institutions treat these companies as though they were the god of financial information. Many victims don't even seek their credit information, as they have too many other things on their minds. If they're like me, they'll feel angst about finding out the results and a fear walking into a bank to request a loan. Because we get refused over and over again, we feel humiliated and degraded. When I had enough nerve to check my credit rating, I found many serious mistakes that were difficult to correct.

A victim of financial abuse needs a break to get back on track financially, but no such breaks exist. We can't even qualify for a low interest loan. It's the old catch 22: we need a loan to get our credit rating back on track, but we can't get money from a low interest lending agency because of our bad credit rating. That means we need to resort to having credit cards that charge a high interest rate. There's something wrong with this picture that needs to be made right for victims of abuse, who already have enough to deal with without financial constraints, struggles, stress, and added nightmares. We victims seem to be the ones suffering for the crimes of others, while the perpetrators go free. Victims have a difficult time finding closure when there is no justice.

The federal Income Tax Act is also unfair to victims of abuse. In most cases, a woman who loses a husband can get a widow's allowance. She also inherits the assets she shared with her spouse and in many cases, can cash in on a life insurance Policy. She'll also be entitled to funeral expenses from CPP, if she earns a salary. A divorcee, who is abandoned by her husband or has to defend herself in court faces significant personal losses. She can't even claim a tax credit for the cost of the divorce and property settlement. The abuser may use the court as a way of abusing his partner, because he can get away with it. The woman often has to work at two jobs in order to pay the legal costs, and this immediately raises the amount of income tax she must pay. Her take home pay, because of the high legal costs, is not her realistic income that she can claim on the net taxable income line, so she has to struggle for years to pay off the high costs of divorce and may need to resort to high interest loans from loan sharks. This is totally unfair. While a widow may grieve her loss, a divorcee who has gone through years of spousal abuse will also grieve and may even have an emotional breakdown or resort to suicide. This suffering does not speak well when one thinks of the quality of life, Canadians are promised in our constitution.

This, my first book, goes back to the source of my becoming a victim, at the time unknowingly, as I was living life in complete ignorance. During a woman's first marriage or relationship with a man, she doesn't know what's normal, even though she might have high expectations, and the abuse cycle sneaks up on her through indoctrination or emotional black mail by her spouse.

We can break the pattern and live a new life.

What I have learned from research is that in order to deal with the future in a better way, one has to revisit the past and learn how one got to the present. I had to do this, but it took much longer than it should have, mainly because I didn't recognize the signs along the early journey of my life, and I couldn't find the support I needed. I also became a typical victim and acted like one. Thus, I had to break this pattern and also break my silence. This took almost a lifetime for me.

There were many signs!

I can readily recognize the signs now, like my friend and his arrowheads, since I've conducted much research, analyzed my life, and know what to look for. At times knowledge is power and at other times it's a curse. How often of late, have I recognized abusive partners and victims and know what's going on but can't tell them, as they won't listen to me? I can see things now, that others can't, which is hard when others live in ignorance or denial, like I did. The feeling of powerlessness is frustrating and at times even suffocating. Society needs to sit up and listen to learn.

I'd like to give many thanks to all of those who made this book possible. I couldn't have done this without all the counselling, the support of others, and the information I found on the internet. And I definitely couldn't have done this without the abusive men in my life. They taught me so much! I can only feel compassion for those so messed up in their lives that they think of abuse as normal or need to abuse and control others with the intention of hurting them. They, too, have a story to tell.

One special counsellor led me to understand that part of my victim complex was due to what had happened to me as a child and my lack of identity that came from a lack of knowledge about my ancestry. This triggered my quest to find answers to my past, my childhood. To do this, I had to go back in history, to a country that was foreign to me. It led me to understand the true meaning of cause and effect, the chain of reactions. It helped me unveil some deep secrets of my past that unknown to me, impacted my entire life. What happened before I was even born impacted my mother, causing certain actions, and these in turn caused my reactions and impacted my life. It ended with me.

A continuous chain of actions and reactions

I also would like to thank all those who stood by me through thick and thin, and for carrying me at times when I couldn't carry myself. You carried me even when you didn't know what was going on with me, but you just sensed that I needed help. You gave me a shoulder to cry on, an ear to listen, a heart to care all of which made me want to live and not die, as in my struggle for survival, death often became a viable alternative to the torture and pain. My wonderful father once told me:

> *"Life is a gift. Appreciate it and what this earth provides for us. Take what you need, and always give back more, making our earth a better place for those who come after you!"*

I thank my beautiful mother, Charlotte, for teaching me honesty, fairness, and integrity. This led me to recognize the difference between right and wrong. I thank my father for his wisdom and unconditional love. He always gave back more and made the earth a better place for many, including me. I wish to carry on his legacy. My pen is my healer as well as my sword; my books will be part of my legacy. I have become a word warrior against any kind of violence and abuse. To get there, I had to understand the human mind and why people hurt and abuse others the way they do. I ask you to join me in my journey of despair and find out how I was able to find hope.

Night without air!

Darkness all around me,
I could not breathe.
A pillow!
Air, I needed air!

I could not get air.
Dirt falling on top of me,
Air, I needed air.
I was going to die.
I was dying,
I was all alone.
Air, I needed air.

PART 1
The Beginning

Chapter 1: She Never Said Goodbye

I believe that I became what I am today at the age of twelve. It all began on a cold, snowy November evening in the late 50s; something happened inside of me that day, something that would steer me in the wrong direction and impact my entire life. It reminds me of *The Road not Taken*. I reached the fork in the road and took the wrong one, but I had no idea what made me take that road.[2] I just did.

Sometimes one gets such a fear in their gut, and their whole world comes, tumbling down, because of something taken away from them. Something important was taken away from me that day, never to come back again. Something that started the internal bleeding, the tears inside of me, that I denied and didn't want anyone, not even myself to see or admit to.

> *Sometimes, when it's too painful to face the truth, we turn to denial.*

I walked into my house and knew instantly something was very wrong. It was obvious by its absence. There was no enticing smell of my "held over from lunch and warmed up" dinner waiting for me and no plates on the table. The plates had always been such a welcome sign for a hungry pre-teen who had just walked two miles after school to get home. It was cold that day and I was freezing; glad to be in the house and anticipating the warmth of a wood stove going. Even that wasn't right; it was too cold in the house. It was

---

2   The Road not Taken, appendix

not like I was used to. Everything was too quiet, and the air had a smell of emptiness to it, a void of the smells I was so used to.

Something was wrong . . . very, very wrong!

It was 4:30 p.m. and already quite dark out. On the way home, I had again encountered the brush wolves, which greeted me on the top of my hill. They frolicked and walked part of the way home with me. They were always so playful and liked my company as much as I liked theirs. I was never afraid of them, but I was nervous to tell my parents about them, as they would be concerned for me. Wolves were something one didn't fool around with, they figured, but I was curious and lonely on the long walk home, and wild animals had never hurt me. They seemed to be as curious about me as I was of them. This was my connection with nature that began very early in life. I always looked forward to their presence and their companionship as much as I looked forward to seeing my family at home. I was the only child at home at the time, and that meant I was a lonely child, with no cousins, no grandparents, and no relatives other than my parents and one older brother, who was already living far away from home. I only saw my friends at school.

I lived on the first level of the Duck Mountains, which could be called living in the bush, a very heavy bush! The Duck Mountains were one of a chain of three mountain ranges that marked the second level of the prairies in Manitoba. The rest of Manitoba was a basin between the mountains on the west side and the Canadian Shield on the east. I called this bush, the "bush bush," meaning it was thick and tangled and hard to walk through. The closest house was a mile away, but my friends lived much farther, and we didn't have a car.

I loved my little family of three and was always happy to get home. Home to me meant comfort, food, and security, which went along with the love of a family. The familiar feeling of comfort wasn't there that night, and everything changed from that day on.

I ran from room to room. "Mamma, wo bist du?"[3] No answer. The house was very clean, as usual and nothing was out of place to indicate where my

---

3 Where are you?

mother could be. I waited a while, but the emptiness permeated my bones and my soul, and I couldn't wait anymore. I knew Papa would be in the barn getting the cows settled for milking time. After I ate, I would go to the barn to milk four cows while he milked two. He only had one hand. Then we'd bring the milk into the house and have another lighter supper, which was more like a snack for me. As father always said, **to be healthy, we should give our supper to our enemies,** but a good breakfast and lunch were important. I didn't eat that night; I ran straight to the barn in a panic. Where was Mamma? She was always in the house when I got home.

Childhood, as I knew it, ended that day.

I had known for a while that something was wrong with Mamma but didn't understand what it could be. For a month previous to this, she had cried and whimpered about a headache and that she was feeling so bad (Ich fühle mich so schlecht!). Father was unsuccessful in comforting her.

I ran to the barn and looked for Papa, who would be cleaning the cows and preparing them for milking. "Papa, wo bist du? Wo is mutter? Was ist los?"[4] He spotted me, and I saw that he had a worried look on his face. "Where is Mamma?" I inquired again, trying to keep the panic out of my voice.

"She went to Winnipeg, to the hospital. She is ill."

"Winnipeg? But that's so far away. When will she be back?"

"The doctor couldn't help her here, so they've sent her to a big hospital where she can be helped and taken care of."

"But what's wrong with her?"

"Ich weiß es nicht."[5]

"But … never mind." I had to think about this. Nothing made any sense to me, as this was far beyond the small world as I knew it. Winnipeg was alien to me. I'd never even seen Winnipeg, only heard of it. I knew it was a big place and that there were things there we didn't have at home. I'd never

---

4   Father, where are you? Where is mother? What is wrong?
5   I do not know.

been more than a hundred kilometres from my home. I had only been to smaller towns like Yorkton and Dauphin, but Winnipeg was four hundred kilometres away, and to a child, that was very far. My world was in Renwer, Manitoba. Winnipeg might just as well have been on the moon for a twelve-year-old who'd never been there.

Why did mother have to go there? We had good doctors in Swan River. Many worried thoughts ran through my head as I was milking. Why so far away? When would she come home? Was she going to die? What would happen to us as a family? Who would do the cooking and the other things mothers do? What would it be like to have no mother but only the two of us, Papa and me? I couldn't even begin to imagine life without her.

She never even said "goodbye."

This absence was a shock, but for a long time she hadn't even known I was there. She didn't hug me or hold me close like she used to. During the last while, she'd been crying all night, every night. I couldn't sleep because I kept hearing her wail during the night and father trying to comfort her. When we went to the doctor, I heard her cry in anguish to the doctor, saying "Please help me; please help me!" Why did she need help? What was wrong with her? I had no clue. All I knew was measles, mumps, colds, and the flu. This was none of them; this was different.

I did my chores, father made OXO cube soup for us, and we ate some bread with goose lard on it. In German, this was called "gänseschmalz." My mother had taught me to read and write in German; she'd been a teacher in Prussia before she immigrated to Canada. I spoke German at home but switched over to English when I went to school.

This was the beginning of the way things were going to be, just the two of us, and neither of us spoke of mother again, as we didn't want to bring up a painful topic. It wasn't the same, that night or all the nights that followed. Mother was gone. There was only father and I to look after the house and secretly wonder what she was doing and what was happening to her. We didn't have a telephone, nor did we have a car. We couldn't go to see her, and she wasn't coming back to see us. She was just gone. For how long? Forever?

Crying on the Inside

I hadn't slept well in a long time. In fact, many nights I didn't sleep at all. That night was one of them, so I started to pray hard for my mother NOT TO DIE. This prayer to God became a nightly thing: "Please, God! Do not let her die!" I would start off with a prayer in German my mother had taught me and then finish with my own prayer of desperation, my plea to God.

Chapter 2: A Superwoman Is Conceived!

That first night with my mother gone was one of severe trauma that would affect me mentally as well as physically, but I wouldn't find out until much later in life. That night started the mystery disease that would progress into something serious. They say losing a parent at age twelve is very traumatic, but I doubt if it matters when it happens. It will always be traumatic, and how we deal with it will steer the course of our future. I didn't deal with it well; in fact, I didn't deal with it at all. I didn't talk to anyone, even Papa, about it. I pretended it hadn't even happened, that this new life of mine was quite normal. I was quite normal. I was more than normal. I was super normal, I thought.

But realistically, I was far from normal. I pushed my feelings away into the far recesses of my mind, or perhaps my subconscious mind, trying to pretend that I was all right. I wore a mask and would become the Superwoman of the future. I could do anything I wanted, I could be anything I wanted to be. I wasn't going to let anything or anyone hurt me; I would just push it all inside of me. I wouldn't cry. I wouldn't talk about it. I didn't let it out! At that time, I also studied the poem "Invictus,"[6] which gave me strength while also making me determined. I was going to be Superwoman, the ***"master of my fate, the captain of my soul."***

Bad mistake!

Christmas that year was lonely and sad. Papa and I tried to put up all the decorations and made a nice Christmas dinner. My brother came home for

---

6   Invictus, see appendix

Christmas, and that was great, but something very important was missing. We opened our gifts Christmas Eve, as is traditional for my culture, and I went to bed early. I cried from missing my mother and then cried even harder thinking she was alone, and because I knew she would miss us too. But no one saw me cry. I cried inside of me deep, deep inside. I knew nothing of what was happening with her or how she was. No one seemed to know. If they did, no one told me. This was so wrong. How does one deal with the unknown? It's easier to deal with what we know, because then we can get a handle on it, but the unknown is so elusive!

Winter went by, and nothing changed in our lives. I had to learn how to cook and wash clothes, which I did when I came home from school. Luckily, Mother had made many preserves the summer before, and often all I had to do was open a jar of something ready to eat for supper. We had chickens we could kill to eat for a Sunday treat, but my chickens never tasted as good as my mother's did. We had a cream separator, so we made butter, cottage cheese and thick milk. All we needed was bread, but I couldn't bake bread. So between the varied diet of OXO cube soup in a hurry or in a pinch, and goose lard on bread, dairy products, and the vegetables and fruit, we fared well.

Father was strained by all of this, and money was very scarce, as prices for farm produce were always an "iffy" thing. Sometimes eggs cost more for the shipping than we got for them, and we had to pay to sell them (transportation costs) rather than make any profit. At times like this, we ate the eggs until we got sick of them, and then we fed them to the pigs or made eggnog for the dog and cats and ourselves. I think father had to send money for my mother's hospital costs. I felt the pinch when I couldn't buy the clothes I needed, so my friends gave me hand-me-downs. This made me appreciate the clothes my Aunt Elizabeth from Germany sent to me in her Christmas care parcel, as they were beautiful and I could wear something new and nice for the Christmas concert. I also loved the marzipan in different shapes that she sent us. It was our only treat.

I loved to go into my father's change and money box, which was a metal cigarette container. He trusted me and didn't mind my being nosy and counting the money; after all, it was a learning experience. There was always a lot of change and many bills to count. I loved to count money! One day in

February, I saw only a nickel in the container. I panicked and wondered how we would survive on a nickel. Times were hard, and the winter was very long, lonely, and grim. Friends didn't offer to help until my mother's friend, Lillian, took some of my clothes to wash. But we were independent, my father and me! This experience taught me to be very independent. I was also proud and wouldn't ask for help for our problems, as Papa and I could handle them. We didn't need help from anyone! But it was nice at Christmas to receive a gift through the Anglican Church, which was donated by a girl in Ottawa. It was a little teddy bear that I hugged every night. It was my comfort when feeling so alone and afraid.

Spring arrived, but nothing changed. Mother wasn't home, but life had to go on. I went to school, came home, and made supper for father and me, and then did my chores. If it didn't get to be too late, or if I wasn't too tired, I'd do some homework or listen to a story on the radio. I loved to listen to Orson Wells read mystery stories on CBC. His voice was deep and haunting. I went to bed at nine, as I had to get up at five. Every night I went through the same ritual and the same prayers, and sometimes I wondered if my mother really was still alive and why she didn't come home. Maybe she had left us for good and my father just wasn't telling me. Or maybe he didn't know. But after a while, this kind of life became normal to me, and my father and I were able to handle it. We were strong; we were invincible. We were Super People, and I turned into a Super Teen!

Chapter 3: The Letters

The letters! It was at this time, that I had opportunities to snoop and find things my mother had hidden from me. I found a stack of letters in German from my wonderful Aunt Elizabeth, and since I could read and write German, I wanted to read them. I had received many letters from her in the past. She and her husband, Gustave, had no children of their own, so she would spoil me with letters and clothes she made, as she was a tailor. She had already sent me a beautiful golden watch, which she said was my grandmother's and my inheritance. I loved the watch so much that I wanted to show it off in school, so I wore it on a chain around my neck. One day when I got to school, I noticed that it was gone. I spent many days hunting for it on the way home and to school, but I never found it. I loved my aunt dearly and wished I could see her, so reading her letters was important to me when my mother was no longer around to keep things hidden from me. My aunt was like a substitute for the mother I didn't seem to have anymore. We all need that nurturing and to know that someone cares about us.

What I read shocked me for years to come, and the content would never leave my mind. One letter in particular made my heart sink into my stomach, and my head feel like worms were crawling all over it. It was in an envelope that had a heavy black border around it, and I learned later that this black border meant a death notice from Germany. I didn't pay attention to the date. This letter revealed a horrible death that my maternal grandmother suffered in a "camp." It spoke of her dying of heartache and sorrow that she would never see her grandchildren. I gathered that her death was sudden and tragic, but that was all I knew. I was so saddened I cried, as I knew then that I had no grandmother at all, and perhaps I never did have a grandparent if they all had died before I was born. Was I even alive at the time this letter was written? This person, Minna Hitz, was my only hope of ever having had a grandparent, and she had died from hertz schmerz![7] Why? What was done to her? What happened in the other world across the Atlantic Ocean, a world I could only imagine from things my father had told me and from what I learned from my aunt?

I put the letter back in the envelope and made it look like I'd never read it. The other letters were also sad, but they were about people I didn't know. So many letters spoke of the tragic deaths of friends or relatives. I had no idea what all of it was about, as I wasn't aware of the Second World War and the devastation it had caused. So many people seemed to have died around the time I was born, December of 1943. And because I wasn't allowed to look into mother's private things, I knew that if she ever came back, I would never be able to tell her or ask any questions. I buried it all within myself, along with all the other feelings of anguish and pain. For many years I wondered if my grandmother died before or after I was born. Did she ever know she had a granddaughter? Would I ever know if I had a grandmother? What would have happened had we met? I wanted a grandmother so badly that I once asked my friend, Ilene, if I could adopt her grandmother as mine as well. I even went to ask this woman and she agreed, so for a while, Grandmother Morris was my "other" grandmother, and I was happy. I loved her house, which had an upstairs, something we never had in our one story "house on the hill!"

But these letters stuck in my mind, never to leave. What camp? A concentration camp, maybe? Why? Was my maternal grandfather, Otto, of Jewish descent? Were my brother and I, children of Jewish descent? I had already heard my grandmother was from near Russia and of Mennonite descent, so would being the widow of a Jewish man have been the reason for her demise? Was my grandfather a Jewish banker? I already knew he was a banker and a prominent business man! To keep my sanity, I found comfort in playing the piano. By the time I was five, my mother had already taught me to read and write in German and to play the piano. I was to become a child wonder, she thought, as she entered me into talent shows to play the piano and to sing "Jingle Bells." She played as well and always won the top prize; whereas I once

---

7   Heartache.

fell asleep on the stage while singing "Jingle Bells" and jingling the bells with the song. At six, I asserted my independence and quit taking piano lessons! My mother never argued, but I would play what I knew when she wasn't around. I was already a rebellious kid so becoming independent later wasn't hard for me. I had a mind of my own, and I marched to my own drum beat!

I loved listening to my mother play. I thought she was a genius. Her music could melt a person's heart! I didn't become the child wonder she had hoped for, but when I turned twelve, I started practicing again. This time I wanted to play, because it was one of my healing and coping devices … or was I doing it as another way to try to please her? By the time I went to high school, I started taking lessons again from another teacher, who put me into Grade 4 piano. I learned at that time that the upright grand piano at home that I was practicing on had been the first thing my mother bought when she came to Canada. It was the most important thing to her. I took comfort in this, and it made playing more important to me as well. If she ever did listen to me play, I wanted to surprise her with how much I had learned. I realize now that I was always trying to please someone, maybe in response to feeling abandoned and not loved. I wanted to work my way into my mother's heart, and this carried on to the men I later became involved with.

Our childhood often determines our future, what we want to be or what we don't ever want to be.

Another distraction for me was learning to sew. I found a few dollars, bought some material, and was given a pattern. I followed the instructions and made myself a jumper with a jacket. Could I have picked anything harder to sew for my first self-taught sewing project? I hated what I'd made and hardly wore it, but this was the beginning of my effort to learn on my own, with no mother or teacher. I also started to draw and drew pictures of animals, which I loved so dearly. Then I learned to knit and crochet, all designed to occupy the time so I wouldn't feel lonely. All distractions! But they were good, positive ones.

I always had a vivid imagination, so on my way to and from school, I'd recite many stories in my head about animals, teenagers in love, and detective stories, so wild an imagination! I never wrote any of them down, so they're forever lost. I read a great deal as well, which might have triggered the stories. Sometimes my favourite cow got to hear them while I was milking her. I spoke them aloud, but anyone else would have thought I was insane. The cow just seemed mesmerized by my monotone, calm, and soothing voice, so she didn't kick the pail over when I was milking her. Everything had its purpose.

The loneliness and personal growth led to creativity and stimulation of other recesses of my mind as a means to cope with the emptiness and the crying inside of me. They say that out of everything bad, comes some good, and this was the good, the self-taught lessons I was able to use later when I made my own clothes, learned to draw and paint, and mastered new songs on the piano. And now I'm writing books about real things that could happen, not imaginary things anymore. I never dreamt then that I would be writing this book. Yet here I am!

I heard rumors about my mother getting shock treatments for a nervous breakdown, but again I didn't know what this meant. No one explained this or anything to me. I wasn't sleeping well at all, and schoolwork started to get harder for me, but I was still at the top of the class, even during those hard times. I so wanted to please my parents, especially my mother! I wanted to be the best in everything, always driven by something I didn't understand at the time. It was the beginning of my becoming Superwoman. I could do it all. I was the best! I was strong! I could handle everything! I started to defy the world and challenged it to test me. I was ready for it! I was ready for anything.

I had truly become the master of my fate;
I was the captain of my soul!

This was also the beginning of my double life. I started doing twice the work an ordinary person would do. I was the wife, my own mother, a student, and a helper for my father on our small mixed farm. I got used to carrying more than my share of the load at twelve, something I would do for the rest of my life. It was expected of me. I expected it from me, so I had to do it. This made the Superwoman emerge even more as the super teen and a fool.

The more you learn to do, the more is expected of you!

People like me are easy to use and take advantage of, but I didn't know that at twelve or thirteen! I turned thirteen in December. I was a teenager now! I had no fear or knowledge of what that meant, and no mother to teach me. Before she had left, she put a box wrapped in brown paper on my dresser, saying I would need these soon. Curiosity made me open it. In it were pads. I knew it was a Kotex box, and one month after she left, I got to understand why I would need them. One night I woke up, and my bottom sheet was red. Oh my God, I was bleeding. I figured out a way to fasten the pad to myself and then went to school determined to learn more about this "girl" stuff. There were books in the library that explained what can happen to young girls as their bodies change from a girl to a woman.

We girls would huddle in the cloak room and look at these books. We had to be so secretive, since talking about this openly was taboo! I learned about menstruation this way, not from my mother. I started menstruating in December, just before my thirteenth birthday. After that I was afraid of boys, as I didn't want to get pregnant and be forced to get married like some of the older girls in our school! I learned from the books that once I started to menstruate, I could conceive a child. Scary stuff!! A girlfriend gave me a small cup bra to wear, so I was set to be a woman now. Super child was ready to fully emerge out of the cocoon as a woman, as Superwoman.

Chapter 4: She came back

At the end of May that year, I was in the barn milking the cows. It was lighter now at night, and as I was milking, a shadow fell through the door. *Mother!* She was back, and she looked wonderful and well, not like I had expected her to look if I ever saw her again. She said "hello" and that she was home for good now. I was so happy, and everything seemed to be all right again. I had a mother, and we were a family of three again. I could go back to being a teenager and forget the mother role. Who wants to be an adult when they can be a teenager? Growing up was so overrated! Wow! Double wow! Life was going to be great now.

But everything was not all right.

This was only the beginning of what plagued me for many years to come. Mother was fine, but not the same person I used to know. She was colder, more reserved, and less loving…far less loving. She was like the talking doll I once had, doing and saying things automatically. I started curling her hair, as she had it short for easier management. It used to be waist length, done up in her special "do," one that I couldn't figure out. It always looked neat, and now it just looked short. After she came back, I noticed a hollow in the back of her head on the left side as I was curling her hair. I asked about it, and she told me that she'd had surgery while in Winnipeg. I never thought to ask why or what was done to her. At that time, it wasn't important to me, but it might have been far more important than I could ever imagine at thirteen. I would always wonder what really happened to my mother, and why she suffered the mental breakdown, which we sometimes call a meltdown. What triggered it, and why did she treat me differently afterwards? What was the surgery for? What part of her brain was removed to cause a hollow in her head? The feeling part? It would be many years before I found the answers to these questions.

I seemed to remind her of someone, as she would stare at me sometimes, as though trying to figure out who I was. Who did I remind her of? I often wondered about this. She would also look at my brother this way, but I could understand this, as he was starting to look like my father did when he was younger. But me? I looked like no one! My father, mother, and brother had the bluest eyes I'd ever seen, while I had blue eyes with a brown ring around the iris, and that totally wiped out the true-blue look. They had darker hair, and mine was platinum blonde. They had nice complexions, and I had freckles! I got sunburns, while they tanned nicely. Who in the world did I look like? I had no idea! This singled me out and made me "different." It wasn't until many years later that I would find out how different I was, and how I was one in five hundred for this and that, or one in a million, etc.! I was certainly different! Or was I just unique? I liked the connotation of "unique" better than "different."

Chapter 5: A New Role in My Life

At the age of thirteen, I took over the role of mother, and when my mother came back, I became her mother in many ways. I wasn't given a choice in this; it was just the role I had to take, as I was the only one who could From that time on, my father and I took care of my mother. It wasn't that she couldn't function in a normal way, there was just something missing, something intangible. There was no sign of feelings, of a soul, of depth. To the outside world, all seemed normal and right, but something had happened to her, something was lost that would never come back. This "something" led to other problems in the future and would change the destiny of our small family in Renwer, Manitoba.

It was hard on all of us, but probably hardest on my father. He was the provider, and when the hospital and doctor bills came, it cost him $10,000. Medicare as we know it today didn't come into effect until later. He was a farmer, so it took a long time to pay off these bills. As a result, we had to live frugally and off the land. I often remarked that the only thing we didn't use from the pigs we butchered was the squeal! We would make grits and blood sausages using the pig's gut for casing. We spent many hours blowing warm water through the gut so it would be clean. We had a special grinder and we made headcheese out of the head and even used the tail for soup. Father smoked the hams and bacon in his special walk-in smoker. The smoked hams were my favourite. It all tasted so good to me. We also made cottage cheese and special thick milk out of the skim milk. I had to churn butter, and we used the buttermilk in baking and for pancakes. The down off the geese was made into feather ticks that kept us warm and cozy on cold winter nights. Nothing was wasted.

We could never afford luxuries, such as television or running water, but we were able to get hydro and a telephone when I was older. Father had to work harder than ever, cutting pulpwood in winter and trying to make more land to sow into crops. He had lost his hand in a sawmill accident in Bowsman, Manitoba, before I was born, so I would joke and say he achieved things "single handily." But he survived. We all did, and in time, I grew up and was on my own. But while at home, I often became my father's other hand. Superwoman was now fully developed and ready to become my persona in numerous ways.

Chapter 6: Where it all Began

What happened to my mother when I was twelve began much earlier in life, but I didn't know it at the time. What I did know came from sources no one ever told me about, such as my Aunt Elizabeth's letters, including the "fatal" letters that added impact to my already changed life and also traumatically impacted my mother's life. At least one of my mother's secrets was out, and she didn't even know about it. All I was allowed to see were the beautiful photos of her childhood, all organized into neat photo albums. Putting those albums together was my mother's project on cold winter nights.

What I read in my Aunt's letters that fateful day went back to a time before I was born to a place called Prussia and a city called Marienwerder. I knew that name from the back of an oil painting that hung on the wall of our small living room. It was an icon of some sort and obviously meant something to my mother. I loved to hear my mother say "Marienwerder," as she could roll the "r" off her tongue better than anyone else. I loved her annunciation and her German. She sounded so intellectual. She'd been a professional in her homeland, and in Canada she was a wife and a mother.

I loved looking at the photos and making up stories in my head about my family to fill the gaps of what I'd never been told. This took the edge off the pain of not having any relatives and worrying about Mother. I once heard my mother say that she was related to a Russian Countess, so I imagined fairy godmothers, rich aunts and uncles, and stately people. The photos also indicated much affluence; after all, my mother had given me the middle name "Elizabeth," after the Queen of England, or so I thought. Or was it after her sister, Elizabeth? Even though we were poor, I dreamt of going to visit my relatives, who I was sure still lived in castles and had servants. Father had a photo of the Airlie Castle on the wall, which he said was the home of my ancestors on his side, the Ogilvies. A castle in Scotland! Wow! And we had a coat of arms, double wow! Only lords, kings, and princes had a coat of arms. We had to be royalty! Or so I thought. To a young girl, this was exciting, and it helped me get through the lonely times of having no other family in this country. This was my story, as I imagined it. It only had figments of truth in it, and I wouldn't learn the truth until fifty-three years later.

My image of my relatives also came from overhearing snatches of conversation between my mother and her best friend. I was a nosy little girl very nosy, or very curious! My mother warned me that I'd have nose troubles if I didn't stop sticking it into things that were none of my business! I now reckon this put a curse on me for what happened to me, fifty years later! I ended up getting skin cancer on my nose and had to have plastic surgery to replace half of my nose with skin from behind my ear. I would laugh later and say my mother jinxed me.

The story as I imagined it began 1931 in East Germany (East Prussia) in early November. A majestic and stately lady, who could have been a countess or a queen, held her two daughters tightly to her heart as she told them how much she loved them. Her name was Minna Hitz, a recent widow, and her daughters were Elizabeth (Lusch) and Charlotte (Lottie). Charlotte was my mother. In this photo of the Hitz family taken in 1928, Minna is in the back between her husband Otto and her other daughter, Elizabeth. My mother is in the front middle with two friends.

In the near future, Minna would lose more but for now, she had just buried her husband, Otto, in September 1931, and was about to lose her eldest daughter, who was going to Canada, a land so new, unknown, and far, away. Would she ever come back? Otto had died of a massive heart attack but had he lived, he would have been heartbroken at that moment, as Lottie was his favourite of the two girls. She was his double in many ways. He was a well-loved man of great stature, a banker, provider, and father who couldn't show feelings; therefore, his ghost stood in the shadows as he watched the three strong but emotional women cry as they talked about Charlotte's departure to a new country. Did the news of Lottie's decision to go away cause Otto to have a sudden heart attack in September 1931? After all, he was about to lose his favourite daughter! A couple of months after his death, the ship was waiting in the harbour and would soon leave for Halifax, Canada. Charlotte turned to leave, only looking back once to wave sadly, and then she left to marry a man she'd never met, a man who was also of Prussian background and now a farmer in Canada. She would become a Canadian citizen when she married Ernst Ogilvie.

Lottie hadn't married up to that point, as men were scarce after the First World War. She was a beautiful, proud young woman whose wealthy parents had the means to send her for schooling in the twenties to take up the profession of a leheren (teacher). She'd lost the man she'd was engaged to marry toward the end of the war, one of the many casualties of World War One. She loved her family and her students, but a part of her wanted a family of her own, and this wasn't likely to happen in Prussia, as she was already thirty-one years old. The ad in the Memel paper that her friend Frieda had shown her sounded interesting, and the adventure would be great. Frieda Ogilvie had placed an ad in the Memel paper for her brother, Ernst, in Canada, looking for "eine gute Deutsche frau object, matrimony!" Frieda, this man's sister, was a likeable young nurse, so Ernst couldn't be all that bad. He had a farm in Canada and wanted a wife, and Charlotte wanted a family and a country life, something she, the city gal, had always dreamt about. Here was her chance. Little did she know at the time, what a wise decision it would be! Who could predict that there would be another world war in Europe that would take away the country she'd grown up in! All she knew was that she had already survived one war, and she'd seen the damage done to her country and the toll it took on her father's business, the family wealth, and her mother.

Charlotte was Canada-bound and on a long journey across the Atlantic, which involved sea sickness and another sickness of loneliness, as she was already missing her family and wondered if she'd ever see them again. Charlotte also worried about her mother, who had just lost her husband. Would it suffice to have her sister, Elizabeth, take care of Minna? Charlotte also wondered about the man she was going to marry. What would he be like? She knew he'd been a soldier in the First World War and had been captured by the Russians in 1915. He was a POW for five years before he was released. He survived while his four brothers and father all became casualties of the war. His sister, Frieda, had shown her photos of this man, and he looked so serious but also handsome in his own way. He had kindly eyes. She would find out in a month how her new life in the New World would be so different from her own. She was to become a pioneer along with her soon-to-be husband, Ernst.

Ernst was from a neighbouring town in Prussia called Memel[8] not far from Konigsberg. His father owned a large farming estate, which had been sold after the war for the "price of a calf," my father told me, as the German money was devaluated to nothing.

Max Ogilvie was a high-ranking officer (a major) in Kaiser Wilhelm's army. He had blown his brains out after losing four sons in the First World War, while his oldest son was taken as Prisoner of War. Knowing that the war had been lost for his country and that he might be imprisoned may also have been factors that contributed to his committing suicide. The war ended officially on November 11, 1918. He had taken his life just a few days earlier, on November 2. Even though both Max and Ernst had won the Iron Cross for bravery, the war had taken much from them all. Ernst and the 17 men under his command were captured by the Russians, in 1915 while being on the Eastern Front. After the war ended and POWs were released, Ernst came back to emptiness, with no life to look forward to. His fiancé had married another man, so he felt the need to start a new life at age thirty-seven. He had a German friend in Renner, Manitoba, named Rudy Deering, and he thought this might be a good place to start a new life. Immigrants needed a sponsor in Canada, and Rudy was willing to do this for him. Ernst knew much about agriculture, as he was a foreman in his father's farm estate, so farming in Canada sounded attractive, and farmland was cheap. The brochure he'd read, invited farm people to Canada, and it sounded very attractive indeed.

He packed his belongings in a trunk and boarded a ship bound for Halifax, Canada, in 1928. Little did he realize a depression was about to hit, but he was ready to make farming his dream come true in the land of milk and honey. He brought his most precious treasure with him in his trunk-a small, folding leather wallet holding photos of his brothers and father. He carried it close to his heart his entire life. I inherited this treasure, to keep safe for as long as I live. I never knew the names of my uncles, as they'd been casualties of the war long before I was born.

---

8   See Appendix for the map of Prussia

Crying on the Inside

In the above photo, my father is centre bottom, and my grandfather, Max, is bottom right. My father was the eldest of the sons, so they are arranged from the youngest to the eldest, starting left top and going down to bottom right. There was only a year between the five sons. The youngest member of his family, the only girl, Frieda, wasn't included in this photo of the soldiers in uniform. Both Ernst and Max are wearing the ribbons, signifying that they had been awarded the German Eisernes Kreuz (the Iron Cross) for bravery in the First World War.[9]

---

9   See Appendix for picture of the Iron Cross of 1914

When Ernst arrived in Canada, life wasn't easy as he made his way across the country by working as a farmhand. The owners weren't always kind, he said and some used these immigrants to their advantage. He got as far as Swan River, Manitoba and had little in terms of money, because many of the farmers expected the immigrants to work for food, and few paid them any cash. When he arrived in the small town of Bowsman, he applied to work in a saw-mill, where he was paid better. It was a union job, and the benefits were good. One day in his attempt to pull out a log, his hand was pulled into the saw instead, and all his fingers were cut off, leaving only his thumb and part of his left hand. He almost bled to death but survived this ordeal. When we would go for walks, I'd hang onto his thumb, which was all he had left of his left hand. This was normal to me. It was only when I went to school and was asked about my father's missing hand, I realized it was not normal, and then asked him what had happened to him.

The compensation for the accident was a $1,000 lump sum payment and $10 a month for life. This was good, as it was the money that bought the homestead near a town called Renwer, where his friend, Rudy Deering, already had a farm. Ernst bought a half section of land on the first hill of the Duck Mountains. This land had good rich soil and plenty of water and trees, so he could run a sawmill off his land in order to build his house. The sawmill was used to cut the lumber for the house he built. Then he was ready for a family, a wife, and a future.

Charlotte Hitz was his future. She was a lovely blue-eyed woman, with eyes that would burn right through you. I always found them haunting. She was both a happy and a melancholy woman, with a warm kind of love for family and friends. The couple married in early December 1931, a month after Charlotte's arrival in Canada. A son, my brother Gerhard, was born in 1932. A second son was lost at birth, and twelve years later, a daughter arrived, so the family was complete. The daughter was me.

Little did she know that her whole life would be devastated twenty-five years later by a surgery that would take this warm love away, along with all her feelings, leaving her an empty shell of the person she was in 1931? This surgery was to impact her life, her daughter, and her husband, but this wasn't known yet. This was only the beginning of Charlotte's life as she knew it. However, the beginning played a major role in the end.

Crying on the Inside

The day they took my mother away in 1956, they also took away my youth and my chances for good relationships with future husbands, as well as with my mother. I didn't know that at the time. What happened to her while she was away for seven months? No one really knew, not even my mother. The Winnipeg Health Authority destroyed any records going back to those years.

Chapter 7: Needs Unmet!

I tried so hard to please my mother after she came back from Winnipeg in 1957, always trying to find the love and approval I'd known before she'd gone away, but I couldn't find it. This only made me try even harder in school, sports, the church, in every possible way. I was always competitive, and I was the best. But this didn't matter to her; she never once praised me or let me feel good about myself. I never felt wanted or approved of; I was just someone living in the same house as my mamma and papa. This made me feel sick inside; I was so lonely and needy. I had no grandmother or sister to nurture me, and it seemed like I wasn't capable of nurturing myself. Super Teen did have her limits, even though she didn't admit to them. So I grew up in a cold home, with only my father's warmth in it, and I did what I was told to do. School became my focus, along with piano lessons, and there I strove to be the best again … always the best, the Super Teen, to someday grow into the Superwoman who would eventually break down and fall!

I so needed a mother! Super Teen, Super Adult, needed a mother! A poem grew out of my head many years later, as the crying inside of me would never stop! The neediness in me grew as I reached adulthood. Missing a woman's love, I turned to my mother's best friends and messengers, who were like nuns, from the Anglican Church, to be my guides and mentors. Lillian Klein, my mother's friend, taught me how to cook and make things, which helped me realize that I enjoyed what a woman's role could be. Mrs. Morris, my friend's mother, also made me feel mature, as she wanted me to make sure her daughter, who was younger than I, was in my care. She trusted me more than my mother did. My own mother didn't want me in the kitchen, as I might ruin things, so I never went there. At home, I was to bring in wood, milk the cows, work in the garden, and, on Saturday, dust the furniture and wash the floor. These were chores and no fun for me. I hated dusting! I didn't understand why mother felt this way towards me as there was little communication between us. Later, I wished I'd been the one to open up conversations, so that I could understand my mother and what she was going through. But that never happened, and I take responsibility for some of it.

Suddenly, I was Grade Twelve, and I was ready to choose a career. I went to see the messengers from my Anglican Church for some advice. The messengers were the ones who held services in small communities like Renwer, in the place of a minister. My mother told me not to marry a farmer or become a teacher, but she never told me why and I wasn't to find out why. The principal of my school, Mr. Hanson, called me into the office one day and told me that I could become a teacher or a nurse. I hated blood or seeing people hurt, but thought I could become a missionary teacher and help people in the Third World. First I had to get my teaching certificate, so applied for Teacher Training at Brandon College in 1962.

Teachers' college tuition and residency cost me a cow and a calf, which I had to sell for the money. My father gave me a calf, earlier, which became a cow, and had a calf, so I had this for my expenses at college. But it wasn't enough, and by February. I had to borrow $300 or I'd have to quit. I told the administration about this, and one of the administrators, Betty Gibson, lent me the money to finish college.

It was there I met my friends who would become friends for life. Gladys and Joan were the ones I hung around with, and they made my year at Brandon Teachers' College, pleasant and a lot of fun. I lived on the top floor and they lived next to me. We had to go down four flights of stairs, which curved around and around. I sometimes negotiated these stairs at an escalating speed if I missed a step at the top. There is no stopping once a person is going down the stairs on their butt, and the speed increases significantly as one goes around and around the spiral staircase for four levels to the bottom. The force of gravity! I did this twice while there. I always had problems with stairs and didn't know why until much later, as this was one of the symptoms of my "mystery disease." Stairs were not my thing. I was to meet the other symptoms later! They were lying in wait for me.

I graduated with the second highest mark that year and two medals for excellence in Music and Primary Methods. I was out .75 for the top gold medal for that year, only a measly .75 lower than my competitor, Ruth! I had tried so hard, but I didn't get the gold medal of excellence I was striving for. Nevertheless, I was so proud, and I wanted some recognition from my mother; after all, I was the second best of around eighty students. My father had sent me a lovely pearl necklace and ring set as a graduation gift, along with a beautiful card. She brought me nothing! She came to my graduation, stayed with me in my room at college, and never once praised me. I was devastated, as I so needed her praise and approval. I had worked hard to earn it. I'd even taken a correspondence course so that I'd have a year of university as well as my teaching certificate by the fall. It wasn't necessary for becoming a teacher at that time, so I was going a step ahead, going the extra mile. She should have been so proud, but she said nothing to her Super Daughter, no praise at all. I cried myself to sleep after the graduation ceremonies! I had a difficult time even talking to her! What was the point of being a Super Daughter if you're not even recognized by someone as important to you as your mother?

The Anglican Church messengers told me of a place where I could start teaching, an Indian Reserve called Moose Lake. It was a Northern fly-in post. I applied to Archbishop Norris for the position and went for an interview with him at the Brandon Diocese. I got the job and was ready to go and begin my new life, and my new adventure, as a missionary teacher.

As before, I again strove to do my very best, but the first year was very difficult. I was ready to quit teaching for good and try another career, like my friend and colleague, Dorothy, had done. She took up nursing. But after the second year, I began to get the knack of it. As a teacher, I also worked my way through university and got my B.A. and B.Ed. degrees through summer school and correspondence courses. Father was still paying off his loan from 1956 and trying to handle the farm in his seventies! He finally sold out and moved himself and mother into a house in Swan River in 1964. Mother was happier there, as she could socialize with friends, have a nice house in town, and once again, be the city woman she'd been in Prussia.

Crying on the Inside

In 1964, I was asked to be a bridesmaid at Joan's wedding in Deloraine. She was marrying an RCMP officer so he, along with his best man wore the red serge uniforms. I was to reconnect with Gladys in Moose Lake after I'd invited her to apply for Dorothy's job. As I worked on a reserve, I went to my parent's house in Swan River, for school holidays and helped my father and mother, financially with decorating, their new house. I bought them furniture and helped make it comfortable for them. Mother never warmed up to me, but we did get along and didn't argue as much as when I was a teenager. I got along better with her when I moved out than when I lived at home. Even when I went home to visit them, the longest I could stay was three or four days before the old tensions came back. I resented her for things she would say to me. She was always critical, never praising. I'd been deprived of praise since my childhood and throughout most of my life, so it became ingrained into my subconscious mind that I was worthless.

The illness that plagued my mother in 1956 would come back from time to time. She would sink into states of depression from which she couldn't come out on her own. Father would phone me in desperation, as he didn't know what to do. I'd help her pack her bags, make arrangements with a doctor, and take her to the Brandon Mental Home, which was what a psychiatric ward was called in those days. There she would get help. In less than a month, I'd be able to take her home again after they adjusted her medications, and she would be better. This happened about twice a year. No one else could take her except me. She knew whenever I arrived that it was time to go. We'd pack her bags and drive off to Brandon. She seemed disillusioned, which made it difficult to talk to her during the six-hour drive to the hospital. I'd feel anger seething inside of me. It was hard to stay calm and be nice to her. I wanted to scream at her, tell her how hurt I was, but I couldn't, as after all, she was a sick woman, and I had to look after her. That was my duty as a daughter. I didn't have to like it. I just had to do it.

At times, she would scold me for being such a terrible and mean daughter leaving her own mother in a camp! I couldn't understand this "camp" thing, but when she called me Lusch, her sister's nickname, I knew she had gone back to a time in her past. I didn't understand, so I was brave but hurting inside. I was trying so hard to help my mother and please my family and I was being scolded and called a bad daughter. This was unfair.

The "camp" thing reminded me of something I'd read when I was only around twelve years old and mother had gone to stay in the Health Sciences Centre, at their Psychiatric Ward. One of the forbidden letters from my dear aunt always haunted me. I remember reading in this fateful letter that my grandmother, Minna Hitz, had died a horrible, heartbreaking death in a "camp." I wondered if that camp had any connection with the "camp" my mother said I was taking her to. When looking at the hospital in Brandon, it did look like the camps I had seen in my mother's photos. What was going through her mind when she called me Lusch? Was she reliving some traumatic event of the past? And if so, what was it? I wasn't to find out until many years later when it was almost too late.

It's never too late until it is too late!

I never did get what I needed from my mother. She later had a stroke and became permanently depressed and had to be looked after by my father. That was a full-time job. When he couldn't do it, I helped out as much as I could. I noticed that something was missing in her eyes, which were often blank, and she seemed emotionally dead. When a letter came announcing the death of her sister, she showed no hint of emotion, no sadness, no grief. *Nothing!*. I didn't understand what had happened to her, and I wished I could talk to her, or to someone, about it, but instead I kept it all inside. I didn't think my father knew the answer, and I didn't want to hurt him anymore than he was already hurting from her being so mentally ill. I knew he loved her, and that made me respect and love him even more. He was a good man and my hero.

I couldn't talk to my mother; I carried this pain inside of me for the next forty years. My mother carried her secrets to the grave in 1987, and I never did get that approval, I so needed. Then it was too late for her to tell me why she treated me that way. I made the funeral arrangements for her, as I had done for my father three years earlier. I loved my father so much and didn't really know if I felt anything for my mother other than frustration, but I cried harder at her funeral than at my father's. Half a year later, I went for a long camping trip with my beautiful collie dog, as I needed to come to terms with all the grief and to deal with my own marriage relationship, which was also hurtful. I had to try to make sense of it all. I needed some closure, a relief from the pain. But nothing was resolved, as we hadn't talked. I should have done this before she had the stroke, instead of being too proud. But I had taken the wrong road of stubborn pride, of being invincible and not attending to my cry for answers. Instead, I pushed it all into a lump deeper inside of my subconscious mind, as my other mind couldn't handle it.

Communications are the most important thing in the world! Nothing should block them.

Did my mother, who seemed such a warm loving person in her Prussian family photos, really hate me that much? Why did she treat me the way she did? Somehow, I felt the answer was with my grandmother, wherever she was buried or had died. Sometimes our greatest fear is discovering the truth, as it may hurt us more than not knowing. I was to find my answers in the future. The truth has always had a way of finding me and find me, it did. It just took far too long.

In 1964, I received an invitation to go to Germany to be the godmother of my Cousin Inge's new son, Peter. I couldn't refuse; this was my chance to meet the very people I used to write to. There I would find some of the answers my mother couldn't provide, I thought. I would ask her sister, Elizabeth, about her. But when I got there, her sister only told me that my mother might feel guilty for leaving her mother behind when she came to Canada. She didn't talk about her mother, and I didn't want to ask. Although I enjoyed the visit, I was no farther ahead about this "camp" thing. Who would I ask? There was no one in Canada to talk to, and the aunt in Germany who had the answers wouldn't or couldn't talk about it either. There was good reason for her to not want to talk, but I didn't realize it at that time. I came back home to continue living with the pain inside of me, not knowing what had happened, not knowing the truth.

I felt that I couldn't deal with the pain until I knew the truth. I went to Germany several times to find the truth but didn't discover anything until 2009 when something very extraordinary happened. When one is always in pain both physically and mentally, it eventually becomes normal, and after a while, one no longer thinks of it. It's just accepted as though it was meant to be. After all, I was Superwoman, and Superwoman feels no pain … does she?

Chapter 8: Inside of the Box

When one is inside a box, its dark, and all one can see is what they imagine is there inside the darkness. That's how I felt. I could only see the little bits of information I'd uncovered in those letters I'd once read and the brief snatches of conversation I'd happened to overhear. The rest was up to my imagination. I couldn't see how much the heartache inside of me was impacting me at the time or how it could impact my future. In the future, it would affect me to a degree that led to a hell on earth I couldn't possibly imagine at that time. My future was made right there, at my little humble home with my family. I was to become a victim, and someday, a victim of abuse so horrible that it would lead to nightmares for the remainder of my life. The paradox was that the Superwoman I had become was victim material to be used, abused, molded, and discarded. Super Woman was to become Super Victim. Was I abused as a child by my mother? That's a matter of opinion. Are cold shoulders, isolation, and lack of approval considered abuse? In a sense they are, as they affected me negatively, but as a child they were normal for me, because that was my childhood … that was my life. I knew nothing else, but at times I yearned for more. It was my father who helped to make up for what I was missing from my mother. It didn't balance things out, but it did tip the scales. He was warm and loving and played with me when I was little. This led me to trust all men in the future, thinking they'd all be like him.

My father taught me much. He took me for long nature walks in the woods, taught me how to shoot a .22 rifle, how to handle farm things, how to drive a tractor, and the many values I would never forget. He filled in the gap, so things were all right in a sense, but were they really?

There was something huge lacking in my life, the female image and role model. I felt I only had a brother and a father, so I became a tomboy, which is easy when one is living on a farm. I did the outdoor chores, and I went on long walks in the wilderness. I tried to learn how to trap animals, and I carried in the wood, drove farm machinery, and climbed trees. But at twelve, things changed as womanhood came with a vengeance one winter night when my mother was away. I was a woman now and needed to deal with that as well, and my father couldn't tell me anything about it. So who would?

I had to learn on my own, and this was probably the hardest self-taught lesson I ever learned in my life. My greatest fear was having a baby! I wouldn't let boys close to me, as I knew having babies had to do with sex and boys. I'd get so afraid when boys would follow me around when I was alone, in case I was sexually assaulted and became pregnant. I made up my mind right then and there that I would not have sex until I was married. Some of my girlfriends "had" to get married, and I didn't want that to happen to me! Because I felt I didn't have a mother, I didn't want to be a mother. I wasn't sure I'd even know how to be one.

When my mother returned from the hospital in 1957, she would take her guilt out on me, her own daughter, who would someday become a victim to men who were also taking out their pain on others. This began a vicious cycle of abuse and being a scapegoat, the one to blame for everything others did and felt. No one told me that there could be cruel men who take advantage of women through divorce or physical abuse, or romantic con artists who con women for what they can get out of them. I only had my father and brother as male role models, and they were good men. A lot of the things I didn't understand as a child would take a lifetime to figure out.

Experience is the greatest of teachers.

I dated a number of boys when I was in high school and Teachers' College, but I always got cold feet when they got too close to me. Half way through my year in Teacher's College, I dated my music teacher, and when he got close to proposing to me, I chickened out and cut him off. He was hurt but soon started dating another musician, whom he later married. Then I ended up going out with his friend, a Brandon College student. Again I felt frightened, as his notes and letters sounded so serious, and I wasn't ready for marriage. I left to go to my parents' house for a few days in the summer, which was a form of running away, but he found me and had a school ring ready when he asked for a commitment which I rejected. I felt like I had broken his heart when I said no, and that affected me for a while. I felt terribly cruel and inconsiderate, but I didn't think I wanted to marry him, or any man, for that matter. Maybe I would just become a missionary and never marry.

Years later, I wished I hadn't been so blunt but instead had taken time to think about it, but I wasn't going to be rushed by men into marriage when I just wasn't ready. When I did get to the marrying stage, at twenty-five, I was still a virgin by choice. It wasn't until I was engaged that I allowed a man to be intimate with me. I wasn't afraid at that point, as I knew I was getting married, and a child born from that intimacy would have a home and a family. I was finally mentally prepared to show my children the love I needed from my mother, and I would never let them feel unloved, unwanted, or alone as I had felt.

But my choice of men as I grew older was pathetic. Maybe I didn't choose them … maybe they chose me and set all the right "hooks." When they wanted a relationship, I didn't say no, even though I should have. I fell for their lies and sympathized with them when they used the self-pity "hook" on me. I believe I was targeted because of my vulnerability. I was too trusting, too needy for love and approval, and too ignorant. Perhaps I was a good catch, as I had a career and a decent paycheque as well a work ethic. I also had become a care giver at age twelve. The man I married later was the same as my mother, which may be why I allowed it to happen. I was already a victim, soon to become a Super Victim, always "doing the dance" to win approval but never getting it. I was too blind to see the character traits in those who could never show any appreciation because they felt entitled to what others did for them,

PART 2:
The Signs

Chapter 9: Previews

Night without air!
A pillow over my face!
My God, I can't breathe!

There was something on my neck holding me down on the bed.

I was going to die!
Don't fight!
It's no use!
He is trying to kill me!
Scream!
I can't!
Air, I need air!

I woke up in a sweat. What was I dreaming? I was known to have premonitions or "previews" as I called them. Being a Sagittarian, the fire sign, I was very intuitive but not practical. I had the gift of clearly seeing future events, before they happened. But this was different, this was a dream. Dreams come from our subconscious minds, and they contain important messages if we can read them. They're a connection between the subconscious mind and our other mind. They try to tell us things of importance we need to pay attention to if we can interpret them. In this dream I could feel the pillow held over my face, and I could smell death. What did it mean?

I have never flattered myself as being psychic, or I'd win the lottery by predicting the winning numbers, but I did have this strange gift of "preview," which was often more of a curse, or a pain in the neck, than a gift. I never knew if the preview was going to happen until it did. I would hope something I'd seen in my mind would happen, but when it didn't, I'd be disappointed.

I applied for summer school when I was nineteen and lived at a dorm at St. John's College on the University of Manitoba campus. I had many other nightmares when I first got there, sometimes of worms crawling in my bed, or fires closing around me. This was understandable, as at the time I finished high school, the area where I lived was consumed with smoke from nearby forest fires, mostly around the Cowan area. At the same time, we were plagued by army worms marching through our area in a very wide path.

Worms were my phobia at the time, which started with worms in the rain barrel when I was around eight years old. The army worms would fall off a tree and crawl down my neck as I was walking home from the school bus. These army worms were pale-green ugly caterpillars with the many feet! Even though they didn't bite, they grossed me out! Walking on them and feeling the slippery grease of their crushed bodies was horrific. I couldn't stand them. Then the ultimate of horrors happened one night when my mother picked these caterpillars off her prize strawberry plants and put them into the kitchen wood stove to burn. She forgot to light the fire, and these little monstrosities crawled out, unbeknown to me, during the darkness of the night. I was asleep when I felt something crawling on my back. I screamed! I jumped out of the bed, and there they were! A whole bunch of greasy creatures crawling in my bed! I couldn't sleep there anymore and went into the living room to sleep on the couch after thoroughly inspecting under, around, and inside it! This was traumatic for me, and with the fires too, I could hardly wait to get out of my town and head for the big city, thinking Winnipeg was caterpillar and smoke free.

For years now, I've had problems sleeping--ever since 1956. Because I couldn't sleep, I started reading, books about animal adventures, such as King of the Mounties, and murder mysteries, such as Perry Mason and Nancy Drew novels. I'd get so involved in the stories, I'd read all night. Sometimes I'd get busted and blasted by my mother for reading late into the night, but after a while she gave up on scolding me, as she was too ill to care. When I'd run out of reading materials, I'd hunt down my brother's detective magazines. It was at that time I decided I wanted to be "Mountie" or a "private eye." When I had absolutely nothing else to read, I'd have nightmares about what I'd read. At other times I'd sleepwalk. One time I found myself in my fleece "jammies" trying to get back into the house. I was freezing. I had sleepwalked outside and locked myself out of the house, and it was not a pleasant morning. I tried to stay warm out in the hayloft of the barn in the dark, the place where werewolves and dragons lurked, or where wild animals hunted at night. In my imagination, that is! I couldn't get into the house until my parents awoke, and I didn't knock because I didn't want them to know what I was doing. I got into enough trouble with my mother, as I could never do anything right, so sleepwalking certainly seemed to be something she would scold me for.

My mind was prone to having many imaginative illusions, many fantasies.

But this nightmare about dying was different. There was no reason to dream of it, as I'd never experienced a pillow over my head. And why would I? It was a preview, and I still wonder why I was gifted with this ability to see ahead. Was the bearer of these dreams and previews my self-appointed guardian angel? Was there a message, even as early as then, that I missed completely?

There are many messages, lady, you just can't read them! You've been given a gift; now you need to gain the knowledge of what they can mean so that you can use this gift!

Sometimes I'd see a place in my head that I'd never been to. I could see it clearly but couldn't think of where, or what, it was. The same place and a few others came to me in visions over a long period of time. Had I been reincarnated, and were those places I remembered from a previous life?

> *There is so much we don't know about the mind, and even less about the subconscious mind. There's a whole new world to discover. After our technological revolution will come the new revolution of opening up the human mind and understanding how it works.*

It is a mystery, waiting to be discovered, a door waiting to be opened. The mind has always been intriguing to me, and in time, I'd be even more intrigued by the "criminal mind." after I took Criminology at the University. What made people turn into murderers, arsonists, assassins, thieves, cannibals and child abusers? What was going on in their mind that made them do those things? They surely couldn't think like "normal" people. They had to have their mind programmed to think differently. To understand how they think could help us prevent crimes by retooling and reprogramming their minds! But that's a dangerous experiment, as such reprogramming could encounter the problems of our computer technology, which has led to great things and also to great crimes. It is used and abused immensely.

Chapter 10: The Secret behind Minna Hitz

All of this began in war-torn Prussia.

I was attending my second last meeting of "Victims of Abuse Therapy Sessions" at EVOLVE, a program offered by Klinik Community Health in Winnipeg, Manitoba. It was on this day that I made a brilliant discovery as to why I became a victim. It was my eighty-seventh hour of the ninety hours of sessions I attended in 1987. History is a story of cause and effect. I am White Wolf Woman, which means I am a white person, a wolf person, and a woman. I am a victim of spousal and partner abuse. The pain of not feeling loved or approved of by a mother transformed into seeking approval and love from men who, like my mother, couldn't provide it because of their own pasts. I kept doing the "dance," wanting to be loved and approved of; always doing everything these men wanted of me to get this love and approval. I became the *perfect* victim. I was setting myself up for abuse!

I was also affected by my lack of identity and roots in this country, making me vulnerable and needy for attention from men, who turned out to be abusive and could mold me like a piece of clay.[10] They could do this because I didn't have a sense of who I really was. I found myself being several people at times. Being constantly put down as a human being made it hard to figure out exactly who I was supposed to be. This also lowered my self-esteem, and I started to feel worthless. All the values I was taught became meaningless, as the men I was with, didn't value them. This was all entrenched deep in my heart and soul and didn't come out until I went searching for answers, years

---

10   Clay, appendix

later. By "heart," I mean the feeling part of our brains, as technically our hearts don't have feelings. A part of me was always crying for the truth of who I really was, of what was happening to me, and why it was happening.

I asked myself if it was possible to grieve for a woman, my grandmother, whom I never knew and who may have died before I was even born. There is evidence that the baby in the womb can feel the pain of the mother. Did I feel pain from my mother while embedded in her womb? Was it because I read those letters when I was nosy? Were those letters a part of my destiny that I lost control of. Why, much later in life, would I still cry when counsellors told me how deeply it had hurt me to not get approval from my mother? In the future, I wouldn't be able to stop the torrent of tears. Years and years of repression came out in the flood of tears. Super Woman had a secret weakness, but on the surface she had it all together and was very strong, but even the strong can go down. All of us have our limits.

One photo in my mother's album haunted me as a child and for many years into my future. I knew her name was Minna Hitz, my maternal grandmother. But who was she really, and what was her story? Where was she buried, and what happened to her that was so horrible my mother and her sister couldn't talk about it? The agony that caused their mental anguish and my mother's breakdown in 1956 also impacted me. This secret wouldn't be discovered until many, many years later. But to me, this woman was beautiful, warm, and loving, and I so wanted her to hold me. I wanted to know her and talk to her. She seemed to be reaching out to me, even from the photo, stirring feelings I couldn't even begin to explain. In the future she was to become a well-recognized heroine, but in the meantime, no one could tell me, or would tell me, where I could find her grave or story. But this woman, in her own way, impacted the lives of two other very strong women in a chain of reactions that would end with me; and the agony would stop when the truth was discovered.

Chapter 11: My First Love

By 1966, I was already a new and experienced First Nations teacher and worked in Moose Lake, Manitoba. Men ... who wants them? I knew I should, but I still wasn't ready to get married. I was waiting for the perfect man who would make me want to marry him. And so far, no dice! It's nice to date, but why get tied down? Hell, I was only twenty-three. My mother told me I was getting to be an old maid. Most of my friends were married and had kids, but that was okay. I had a career. I was a teacher, the closest thing to being the missionary I wanted to be. I worked for the Anglican Church the first year, and then continued working for two years in the same community when Frontier School Division took over this school. This Native community was my first mission and only mission job. My girlfriends married and became farm wives and mothers, but where would they go in the future? How dull, I thought! They'll just sit at home, look after the farm, and make a whole bunch of snotty-nosed kids. Who wanted that? I wanted to have a different life. I ended up getting my wish, but at a huge price.

I always felt I was a little different but didn't know why. Hell, I didn't even know my maternal family, other than my mother. Maybe they were like me ... or I was like them? Well, I had no identity, but I always knew I was different. Something in me made me want to get a career and be someone, and not just be a farmer's wife, even though there's nothing wrong with that. It just wasn't for me. Yet this was an anomaly. I had wanted my father's farm and to become a farmer but not a farmer's wife! Part of the old tomboy was coming out, or perhaps I was on the forefront of the women's equality movement. Just because I was a woman didn't mean I couldn't become a farmer.

My father had taught me all about farming. I was his helping "hand," and I could plant crops, make hay, raise cattle, and run the farm machinery. I was always with my father, helping him and avoiding housework and my mother. He was fun to work with.

I didn't drink as a teenager, and I always turned down cigarettes. That's where I drew the line in trying to please others; it's where my intellect and learned values kicked in, as I knew those things were bad for me. Others said my parents were strict, but to me it was normal, and I didn't suffer for it. Perhaps I was a little too protected by my strict parents and not savvy enough about street life. I only knew my own life and my little world, up until I got out into the real world.

After I turned twenty-two, my parents were down on me all the time about not getting married. Why? They didn't get married young? My brother was married, and he didn't look happy. How could I get married when I went with guys but didn't love them? I wanted to love and be loved. I was popular, but men got frustrated when I turned down their offers of marriage. I hurt a lot of guys. I was just a heartbreaker, and I wasn't proud of it. I'd refused three engagement rings by the time I was twenty-two and I'd been a bridesmaid three times. I guess I was born to be different. Father had always said to "get a career" so that I could be independent. One never knows when they'll need it, he said. Maybe men are supposed to look after women, in those days, but who knows what course our lives could take? "It's better to be prepared." Wise words! My father always displayed such wisdom, and I've never regretted listening to him. So why this hurry to marry me off? I wasn't done working on my career. I wasn't ready to tie the knot and have kids. Someday I would be, but not now, and perhaps never.

At times in my future, I wished I had gone for the "never."

There were times when I thought of the man whom I'd dated when I was going to teachers' college, and I wondered where he'd gone, if he missed me, and if he was still single. Whenever I took my mother to the Psychiatric Hospital in Brandon, I'd sit outside of his parent's house but was always too chicken to knock on the door. I had mixed feelings about him. I missed him in some ways, but I wasn't sure how I felt about him. How I felt was a mystery, until one day, years later, I would figure it all out.

But then I met a wonderful, slightly younger Native youth in Moose Lake, who was so nice, sweet, and gentle. His name was Louis. I started feeling things I'd never felt before. We'd go for long walks, talk, and hold hands, and kiss but we never went any further than that. It was a sweet relationship and very fulfilling, taking the edge of the loneliness many white teachers felt on northern First Nations reserves even though we were made to feel very welcome in the community and were thankful for that. This young man wasn't like the other fellows who were constantly writing notes to us female teachers and getting their younger siblings in our classes to bring them to us. He was respectful and shy but at the same time quite brave to want to go out with a white woman. Did I feel love or just a sweet respect and gratefulness to the man who made my empty life there feel fulfilled and happy? He was going to go away soon to attend a trade school, and we would be corresponding. I missed him when he was away and looked forward to his letters. My respect for this man grew because like me, he did not smoke or drink. He also was interested in a career.

But one day I was to experience a culture shock I hadn't expected. I wasn't Catholic, but he was. The Catholic priest and the Anglican minister from my church came to see me to talk to me. Louis had confessed to the priest, who talked to my minster, that he wanted to marry me. They told me to leave him alone, to not go out with him anymore or see him, as he was Native and Catholic. I was Anglican and white, and the two did not mix they said to me.

I'd never felt any prejudice against anyone in my life, and to me, all human beings were the same. To be told this by two high ranking, respected community members hit me very hard. Were they right? Did I not have the right to go with a native boy? I withdrew into myself, and hard as it was, I didn't answer Louis' letters after he left the reserve.

He wrote to me for a while, and I still didn't respond. Then I never heard from him again, only to hear from others that he married someone he met when at trade school and that was the end of that. I often wondered about him and never forgot him, and sometimes I took out the notes he sent me to read them again. I wondered if I done the right thing and if things would have worked out for us had I not listened to the priests. But I also knew I was not yet ready for marriage not at twenty-three! I lost Louis to another woman, but I loved him enough to want him to be happy, and to be happy for him.

Then I met him, the perfect man! Or was he?

I met the man of my dreams, the man I could love and knew I wanted to marry (or so I thought) in Moose Lake, in 1965. He came there with a crew of surveyors. He could dance up a storm, and we danced so well together. We were both from German backgrounds. We suited each other. He was tall, handsome, and a "hunk." His name was Joe, and he had a friend working with him named Brad. Joe was the helicopter pilot, and Brad was one of the surveyors who'd come up to the reserve where I'd been teaching for the third and last year. They were working on a project for Manitoba Hydro. All the single men who came there would end up at the teacherages having coffee with the young single teachers, flirting with us, or just passing the time, as there was not much else to do there.

Joe and Brad spent their evenings with us. We'd talk, go for walks, and dance when there were dances or socials in the town hall. It was so much fun. I was missing Louis less and less. Joe would go out with me, and Brad went out with my girlfriend, Dorothy. He suited her too, and they made a great team. We often double dated. Then they left, and even though I thought I would never see Joe again, I felt that it could be love; it could be the real thing, for keeps. For the very first time in my life, I was ready to get married, and he happened to be there when I felt this way. Finally, I felt like I wanted to be a wife, and have children with a man, a family.

Several of us teachers had come to teach in Moose Lake, and left at the same time. Three years is as long as one should stay in an isolated place, or one will never leave. The reserves and the people grow on us, and we become attached to them. I went to Winnipeg to finish up my Bachelor of Arts degree in fall of 1966, and Dorothy went into nurses' training. Then, lo and behold, we ran into Joe and Brad in Winnipeg again. We continued to double date for half a year.

One night, while on a double date, Brad put his hand on my knee under the table, and I wondered why. He was going out with Dorothy. I would see

Joe whenever he was in town, and we'd go to bars together or hang out with his friends, and sometimes with Brad and Dorothy. Joe and I would hug and neck on the couch but were never intimate. I was still a virgin, as that was what I wanted to be. I wanted the man I was to marry to be my first. Kind of silly, I thought later, but those were my principles, and I stuck by them. I felt I wanted to get serious and told Joe that, one night. He reacted to what I said as though I'd slapped him in the face. He got up and left, and I was devastated by how he'd reacted to what I'd said even though it was said in honesty. At that time, I was not aware that there was something sinister going on behind my back that I was not aware of.

He didn't call me anymore.

After that experience, Brad started calling me to ask me out. I wondered why, but I went, as I was still hurting that Joe had ditched me. I felt like the woman scorned, and that was hard for a vain person like me to take; besides, I was starting to feel something for this other man! Brad and I became an item, and Dorothy gracefully backed out. He told me that Dorothy was too religious for him, and she wouldn't dance or go to dances. I didn't feel for Brad like I felt for Joe, but Brad was so "nice" and fun to be with, so it was okay. It took away some of the pain. He seemed to like me and want me, and being liked and wanted were what I always did the "dance" for.

Brad told me that Joe was an alcoholic and took drugs. That made me feel better about being dumped and also prevented me from making that call I so wanted to make. I felt I needed to get an explanation from Joe for his abrupt departure but pride got in the way. I hated alcohol and drugs, and I never saw Brad drink or smoke dope, so he now seemed like the ideal man for me, and he also loved to dance. So did I!

Get over it, lady. Joe never was any good for you. This man you're now dating is much better. You are lucky to have Joe ditch you.

It was for the best, I thought. That was me trying to convince myself, but I never could … not completely. It was the beginning of deception, a deception that impacted the course of my future, the beginning of the lies and betrayal I never could see until about twenty years later. Many times I just wanted to pick up the phone and call Joe, just to talk, but I listened to this other voice inside of me arguing with that reasoning. I lived to regret this neglect for the rest of my life. "Pride and vanity goeth before the fall!" This pride of mine was so foolish. I was so vain!

> *Call him … don't let your pride stop you. Call him … he wants to hear from you. CALL him! You have to make the first move if you love him. Call him.*

Mixed messages! I was torn and tempted, but, regrettably, I never did call. Brad had made me feel badly by his emotional blackmail in taunting me that I was still in love with Joe, so I had to prove otherwise. I had to prove my love and faithfulness to the man I was to marry.

As I look back at my past now, I realize that I always had signs, or voices talking to me, and now I see that some were evil and some were good. The evil words were from the devil himself. I should have been listening more carefully to the good voice and ignore the evil ones. By making assumptions and not communicating, I never learned the truth, and this also had an impact on my life forever. It was much the same as my lack of communications with my mother and what that did to me. Why was I this way? Why did I really want men like my father but ended up with men who were like my mother and could never give me what I really needed?

I should have swallowed my pride, recognized it for what it really was, and listened to the inner voice inside. If one feels true love, they need to pursue it and not give up so easily.

Chapter 12: "Til Death Us Do Part"

Brad and I went out together for two years. The odd time, Joe would drop in on me, but it wasn't the same. We never talked about things of the heart, and now I realize we should have, as it was there for both of us. How was I to know if we didn't talk? I also thought about the man I'd dated in 1963. I still stopped by his place in Brandon and wondered if he was still single and still cared for me. We never had a chance to really get to know each other, and that made me sad.

Our courtship was sweet, at least to me, with hopes, dreams and anticipations. Brad was into antiques and old cars, and it wasn't long before I also bought into this. He had a beautiful red 1952 MG convertible, which I loved. It had suicide doors and the thirties look. But he sold it to Joe and talked me into buying one myself, a yellow 1953 MG, which I financed and had paid off in two years. When I went to register it, Brad encouraged me to sign it over to his name so that we could save on insurance, he said. I was gullible, but this was one of many signs of what I was getting myself into--the sign of possessiveness. If it was in his name, it was his! I totally missed that first sign. The second one came soon thereafter.

We were in church, one day, which he hated, as he was an atheist. There can't be a God, he told me, or He wouldn't have taken his mother from him at age twelve! His mother had died of cancer. I felt in my heart that I didn't lose my mother at that age, possibly due to my faith and the many prayers I shot up to God. But Brad went to my church with me to accommodate me, a then devout Anglican, baptized and confirmed in this church. As usual, I went up for communion while he remained in the pew. I noticed a frown on his face but didn't make anything of it. When I came back, the frown was still there, and I noted a tension between us. I asked him about it on the drive home, and he told me that he was angry because I'd gone up for communion.

"Why?" I asked.

"You do not belong to God; you belong to me!"

I was shocked at this, but it was another sign of his possessive nature, not just of material things, but of me as a human being.

I belonged to him! Little did I know at the time, but I had become a disposable commodity the day he claimed I was his!

I was a possession already, even though we were only engaged I was his possession to do with as he wanted, to control and use, and when no longer needed, to discard. It's one of the three main signs of an abusive relationship in its first stages.[11]

There was so much I didn't see in him. He was super nice, setting the "hooks" to catch his sucker, which was me. In his eyes, I was a good catch: attractive, smart, hardworking with a well-paying job, and the child of elderly parents with assets and maybe money! Inheritance is a good incentive for a man to whom money means a lot. I was targeted by a "parasite" who planned to live off others but had to hook them first by being on his best behaviour, saying the things I needed hear, and conning me into believing he was a much different person than he really was. I was to believe this for the next eleven years. We got engaged in April 1968.

The masks people wear!

He wasn't the only one wearing a mask. We all wore one at that time. Joe came to see me in Snow Lake when I was engaged to Brad and teaching there in late 1968. We were just friendly and nothing more. We avoided talking about any feelings we might have had about anything, including each other. He wanted to stay the night. That would have worked, as my roommate was gone for the weekend, but I wouldn't let him. We hugged hard and passionately when he was leaving, and the temptation was there to forget the

---

11   Three signs of abuse to watch for see Appendix.

engagement ring on my finger, to forget Brad, and to just succumb to the feelings and the passion. But I didn't and I always wished later that I had. A night of passion might have changed my destiny, but I had to be a prude and faithful to a man who was never faithful to me.

I later found out that Joe had gone to see my family, and my brother and his wife, without him telling me. I wondered why he went through the trouble when he hadn't wanted to be with me two years earlier. They all told me that they thought he liked me, maybe even was in love with me. I began to wonder if he really did love me, but it was too late. I was never the cheating kind, and I had married Brad in August of 1969. So he was the man, I would stay with until "death us do part," or so I figured at the time. Being young and naive, I didn't see the double meaning of those words, but that was perhaps another of the many signs!

Night without air!
A pillow over my head!
He wants it all!
Darkness!
I Scream!
I am going to die!
Air, I need air!

My parents were impressed with Brad and were very happy that we were engaged. We got married a year and a half later. We had a small wedding at a German bar and restaurant in Winnipeg called the Happy Vineyard. It was pleasant and made my parents very happy, as they felt at home with the German ambiance.

"With this ring, I thee wed." I vaguely heard the words as the ring was being slipped onto my finger. In the twenty-nine degree humid air, my fingers were swollen, and the ring refused to slip over my knuckle. Was that another sign? So many signs, so little understanding of what they might mean!

'Til death us do part!

I pushed the ring over my knuckle; I just wanted the ceremony to be over and to get out into a breeze. I was feeling trapped with the humid hot air. The chapel at St. John's College was sweltering, and I felt claustrophobic, hot, and uncomfortable in my long white dress. Getting the ring on my finger would bring the ritual to an end, and I was going to force it and force it, I did.

I can't breathe!

A ring is a circle, which can mean many things depending on one's perspective. A red ring is the circle of life to First Nations people; an enclosed circle means security, strength, and safety, but it can also symbolize a trap and a prison. Gold stands for preciousness, but gold is cold and hard, a metal! I paid little attention to these things. It was my wedding day, the day women dreamt about at that time. It was the beginning of a future, a family, and a fairy tale dream come true. I never thought of the symbolism, of the meanings of a ring, and the words "'til death us do part." This was my day and nothing was going to spoil it! Dance, laugh, and be merry! Don't listen to those voices in your head!

Maybe I should have listened, but it was too late after the vows!

I was to find out that the circle of a ring can represent a "prison of prisons," as I entered this world of entrapment in the sanctimony of marriage, which never meant the same to my partner as it did to me. I would be in bondage for the entire time I spent with him. I became his host, which every parasite looks for. He would suck the lifeblood out of me until there was none left, and then the parasite would seek another host. All I went through was symbolic, and my life reflected the double meaning of the symbols of a simple wedding ceremony. As I sat and prayed in the pulpit before the ceremony began that day I looked up and saw the crucifix, a symbol that Christ had suffered and given up his life for us so that we could be redeemed and have hope. Strangely enough, the diamond on my finger had four points to form the shape of a diamond, but if looked at differently, one could visualize the diamond from inside the four points, and then it became the cross! Everything had a duality. The diamond hard, cold, and beautiful could become a cross, a symbol of betrayal, of suffering, agony, and death. And it did! Later!

"For better or for worse" in life and in death!

The duality of this vow struck me at the time for a second, but the thought soon vanished in the celebration of the moment. I hated the "death" word at that time. It was too dark, when starting a "new life" with new hope and anticipation for a long-lasting love and happiness, as in a fairy tale. I was soon to find out that the dream of every woman's youth could soon become her worst nightmare. We tend to think these things happen to other people, but they can happen to us, a marriage that begins in heaven can end in hell. I never thought about the words "until death us do part," or their double meaning, until it happened!

This marriage vow sounds good, doesn't it? But watch the "death" word! Be warned lady! See the double meaning in this.

I did not listen. Why would I? He was such a nice man, easy going, loveable, sweet, and extremely likeable. He seemed almost too good to be true. I got the feeling he was well liked, and I learned to love him! I had come to love everything about him. He was the man any woman would want, in my eyes. Besides, he was also handsome in his own way, appeared intelligent, and could put on the charm. Watch out for charming men, I was once told. But to be charmed was kind of sweet. He seemed soft-voiced and gentle. Who could foresee what was going on in that mind, what he was really capable of, or the demons that tormented him and stirred up such evil thoughts?

Be careful, things are not always what they seem. People wear masks; look beyond the mask and find out what kind of man he really is! Beware of smooth-talking men, as they are not what they seem. They're out to con you, not love you. Love is only a word, loosely used to set the "hook" for one who is vulnerable and needy for love.

But I didn't know men like that existed. My experience with men up to that point were the role models of my father and brother, and boys I'd gone out with who were sweet, honest, and gentle. I thought all men had to be like that. I'd never been taught that some men could be con artists who would lie, deceive, and even murder to get what they wanted out of others. Men, who are narcissistic, selfish, self-serving, and self-centered. Life is all about them, and every action they take is carefully planned in order to deceive. But I was naive, vulnerable, and too trusting.

Chapter 13: The Illusion of Happiness

In our first years together, we seemed to be so much in love. I worked hard, while he quit his job and started into a cow-calf operation full-time. I cashed in all my bonds, retirement funds, and assets to buy the basic herd of cattle, new machinery, and three parcels of farmland to add to what I "thought" he already had. I didn't do a single thing to protect myself "just in case," as I trusted to the extreme. This was very foolish of me; I was very gullible. I also worked hard to pay off the debts, as I was the only one who could. The farm never showed a profit, but I had a job as a high school teacher, and could pay the bills.

We went a lot of places, lived and traveled frugally. We slept in our station wagon to avoid hotel costs. Our best vacation was to Corpus Christi, where we could park on the long sandy beach and sleep to the sound of the waves coming in, while laying safe and secure in each other's arms. We went everywhere together. We worked together and made mad, passionate love whenever and wherever we could: the back of the car, the hayloft, the bushes, the table, the hayfield, under a bridge, and the station wagon. Any place would do for young love.

Night without air!
My body stark naked!

Suddenly, there were people sitting all around me, staring at me.

I could not breathe,
Or cover myself.

I was totally ashamed and embarrassed and covered my face. When I looked up,

They all disappeared.
I was alone,
So alone,
And afraid!

I woke up in a sweat and suddenly felt alone. No one was around. I was completely alone in this world. I was afraid of being alone! I started shivering all over, as though cold, and then I turned to the man in my bed, my husband, and smiled. I wasn't alone. I had him; I would never be alone, I thought. He loved me just as much as I loved him. Only a few nights ago, when we were about to make love, he'd looked at me, his eyes softening with love. I just melted into his arms, and the night exploded in passion. We were happy together, so why was I having these dreams?

"Dreams are from our subconscious mind; they are messages."

I had no idea what this meant or what the message really was. I couldn't understand this dream, as I felt so secure when he held me in his arms at night. It was great to have such a wonderful man in my life. We hardly ever fought. It was like an eternal honeymoon. We worked hard, but we also played hard. Then it was time to start a family. We tried and tried, but nothing happened. Why, God, Why can I not conceive?

You don't really want kids, trust me. You'll see in the future why you wouldn't want to have children with this man.

But I did so want children, at least two, a boy and a girl, a family. I was even ready to give up my career for farming and raising a family. Foolish, but I was ready to have a family of children who would have his charm, my mother's looks, and my intelligence! No vanity in me! These children would not only be smart, but beautiful! Like me, they would be something any parents could be proud of. I knew that my parents were professionals, skilled, talented, had a great work ethic and a drive to do the very best possible. They had ventured across the ocean to make a life, and that took a great deal of courage. The genes would be passed on through my children, and I knew I'd be a good mother. I learned from what I lacked from my mother how much a child needed nurturing, love, and approval. Our children would never go through what I did!

I lived in a world of trust and worked hard to make things work for us, to make a beautiful and comfortable home, but I was blind to all that was happening around me. I thought back to my father's words, that ***"people and things are not always what they seem."*** I knew he was right; my father was always right, but for now, life was hard, but it was good. I was very happy! We had good friends, and our social life was a lot of fun. With my job, frugality and resourcefulness, we would be out of debt soon, and then we could live a little, go on luxurious vacations and sleep in fancy hotels, have a family or adopt a family, and life would continue to be good.

But the dream of being naked and alone kept reoccurring, and I couldn't understand why. When I'd wake up I'd feel the warmth of his body beside me, and I'd put my arms around him and whisper, "I love you so much. I will never be alone as long as you're beside me." I felt that this love would last forever. An illusion, a fairy tale! A Super Fairy-Tale!

Chapter 14: Ember Ranch Is Born

We worked hard on the farm, the cow-calf operation and our house with so much character. It was a lovely log house. I loved my home, as it was so warm and unique. We had cedar cupboards and walls. I was good at design, and we shared a love for old things, antiques, and wood. We'd been given this log building to take off an island near where we lived. Brad took it apart, brought the logs over the frozen Winnipeg River in winter, and rebuilt it on our lot. It was all so rustic looking, and to complement this look, we had antique furniture that both of us collected and I had refinished into gleaming wood. The house felt good, even if it wasn't finished. I had plans for the veranda, but it never got to be. I loved verandas. They had a warm feel to them, like days of old, and ranch houses always had verandas! My focus was on paying off the debts so we would be debt-free. Then we could save money and do the things we wanted, like build a deck, a sunroom and install a Jacuzzi on the deck.

Dream on, lady. That's what makes life worth living, living for dreams, but also know that this is only a dream, an illusion, and may never come true. However, we can enjoy the anticipation. We all need to have dreams and to believe in them. We can follow our dreams until the day they are taken away from us!

The three of us, my husband, my father-in-law Ralph and I had started a cow-calf operation in the rural municipality of Lac du Bonnet. Ralph's common law wife had left him by then. He already had a basic herd. I cashed in my $4,000 in bonds to buy our own basic herd. We bought twelve heifers to start a herd and put them together with Ralph's, at the farm, six kilometers away. Then we looked for a purebred Charolais bull. This was the beginning of what was going to be one of the best breeding herds in the province. We were part of the Farm Diversification Projects and attended every workshop they offered. This also gave us some free grant money for buildings to accommodate our cow-calf operation. I signed us up for many other projects, such as breeding programs for best record of performance (ROP) cattle, and I took out a lifetime membership in the Charolais Association. From our trip to Texas, I got the idea that a three-way cross, starting with a dairy animal being bred to a bug resistant animal, the Brahma breed from the US, and Charolais would make for performance cattle who gained fast and were toughened to our climate conditions. We bought some Charolais-Brahma cross cows, and in ten years we had a three-way cross. We had Shorthorn and Jersey for milk bred to Angus/Hereford for the beef part, crossed with Charolais/Brahma for insect resistance and size.

We had developed a tough, healthy, and good performance herd, with calves that weighed out at six hundred to nine hundred pounds in fall, when we sold them as feeders to finishing operations. Our cattle were in demand by buyers, and even though the prices were lower in the late 70s, we did better than the traditional Angus/Hereford breeders.

This was fun for me. Being from the farm, a ranch was my dream. I read so many Zane Grey books as a kid, and I would dream of having a real ranch, someday. Now I had one to share with my husband and father-in-law! It was a challenge, and as I had done for my entire life to that point, I did the very best possible, always going the extra mile to be a perfectionist and competitive with the best. And we were. Brad's huge ad photo hung from the ceiling at the Brandon Winter Fair, naming him as one of the young farmers who would carve the future! I didn't need the credit, as I knew my role in all of it, and that made me proud. We were a success, and of course inside of me was always the desire to please my man and be a good wife so that he would love and approve of me!

But cattle prices plummeted to below the cost of production in the late 70s. I worked hard every weekend, every holiday, and every night to make this cow-calf operation work the best it could. But my partners didn't "make hay when the sun shone," as I'd been taught to do. Brad and Ralph did things when they felt like it! Unlike my father, who was also a perfectionist, they didn't check the barometer to see if rain was coming, nor would they go out to the field and bale the hay before it rained and took the nutrients out of it. They wouldn't get up in the middle of the night to check the calving. When a calf is born, it's weak, and it's crucial to be there to either assist with the birth or rub the calf's neck to get out the mucus and stimulate the heart. If it's cold, you need to dry off the calf by rubbing it with a towel to keep it warm enough to live. They wouldn't do these things, so many calves died at birth.

Our calves were born in February, so it could be forty below at night. No calves could survive that cold when so wet at birth. April was another crucial month as scours, a digestive disease, was common amongst calves and highly contagious. This meant certain death if efforts weren't made to deal with it. To be proactive meant making shelters on higher ground to keep the calves dry, or when they started scours, to feed them electrolytes through a stomach pump, along with giving them penicillin shots. Many died at this point, even though I worked hard to save them when I was able to on evenings, weekends, or whenever I wasn't teaching.

But the men did nothing, so we missed the magic number of having an 80 per cent calf crop to sell in fall, which would keep us from losing too much money when cattle prices were low. We usually ended up with a 60 to 70 per cent calf crop, which meant a $5,000 to $10,000 loss every year. Who made up for this shortfall? Of course, it had to be me, as I had a job! I carried the stress load myself most of the time while my partners did what they felt like doing.

I could never understand this. If one was going to be a farmer, why not work at it and make it viable, make it succeed? Where was the pride? Why did the square hay bales lie in the field until winter, to be picked up when they were suddenly needed hay? Then they pulled the bales off the fields on a hood of a car pulled behind a skidoo. These hay bales sat in the fields from July and August through many rains, so they lacked nutrition and were moldy and often rotten inside. This meant little or no nutrition for pregnant moms, who needed all the nutrition they could get. What was so wrong with picking up the bales after making them? There were two trucks available, Ralph's and Brad's, while I drove an old station wagon wreck. So I started picking up the bales myself, using one of the trucks. I could understand why no one would want to pick them up. The bales weighed well around a hundred pounds, far too heavy for a woman to lift. So why make such huge bales if no one wanted to pick them up? What was wrong with making sixty pound bales? One just needed to make an adjustment on the baler.

These bales were far too heavy for me, and I struggled with them. The first ones were easier, as they formed a bottom to the box off the truck. The second and third layers became more difficult. I used every muscle I could; I used my knees to push the bale up to the first level and tugged, pulled and pushed until I got the bales up on the load. Somehow I had the idea that my back muscles would become stronger as I worked, and that soon I wouldn't hurt so much when I lifted up the bales. I found out later, from my doctor, this only works for men. Women are made differently, and the muscles in our back don't get stronger. Stacking them was easier, as I could park the truck in such a way that I could throw them down and then drag them into place. I used my brains, what brawn I had, and my experience from my father's farm to make a nice stack for the winter. When I was finished, I was hurting but pleased that the cows would have fresh alfalfa bales, with tons of nourishment and loads of carotene, so that we wouldn't have the calving problems we'd had before. I'd read up on it, and found out that hay low in nutrition would cause the pregnant moms to delay birth by two weeks or more, so the fetuses often grew too big for easy birth, and thus problems would occur. I was a perfectionist and all had to be perfect with our cow calf operation, as we had the breeding stock. Now we needed the management … perfect management. Super Management! Did this mean I had to do it?

This change in my life was subtle. ***The more I learned to do, and the more I did, the more I was expected to do.*** I had the theory that I "had" to do this if no one else did, as it had to be done! So I took on increasingly more responsibility for the cattle, in addition to my regular job as a teacher. The men, of course, took on less and less, so a fair balance here was way out, and the Superwoman had to take care of it as this human could not. Every time the burden became too heavy for me, I would throw on my cloak and take care of the slack, because if I didn't, ***it wouldn't get done.*** I started to wonder exactly what my husband and his father were doing when so much was left undone. Were they lazy, or did they not care? Were they intentionally dumping more on me, so that they didn't have to do it? Where was the fairness? I didn't complain. I chose to do this in silence, as I couldn't understand an attitude of laziness and wasn't ready to face what I knew, deep inside of me, was the truth.

These men were lazy and I was being used!

I ended up going to the farmhouse and spending the night there so I could get up and check the calving on cold winter nights. I was the one dragging a huge calf inside because it was weak and would die if I couldn't warm it up. I'd use a sack and put one end of the calf into it and then drag it into the house. Sometimes I'd make a fire in the farm house's wood stove and then would rub the calves and give them nitro to energize them. This worked well, as their hearts would start beating and life would come into them. It always made me very happy to save a life. I didn't want to think of why we were raising this beef, and that the males would be someone's "steak" or "roast" someday! I always hoped for heifers, as we would keep the best of them for breeding stock, and they would have a longer life!

In April, I would go and blow electrolytes through tubes into the stomachs of calves with scours, give penicillin needles, dehorn all the calves who had little horns starting go grow, and "denut" the male calves to turn them into steers. We had little elastic bands with an instrument that would do this, and I always wondered if they felt the pain of tight elastic bands around their testicles. This was better than castrating them later, as the knife was wicked and there would be so much blood.

When spring came, there was fencing to do, and in summer, hay to cut. I could work the crimper and the baler, but most of my time was spent cutting the hay and raking it while Brad baled it. Then I would "stook" the bales in a bunch and pick them up later whenever I had the time. The "stooking" kept them from getting wet and moldy inside, as the stook formed a little roof. At harvest time, I could use the swather and sometimes even the combine to thrash the crops for feed in the winter. The only farm machine I didn't use was the round baler, which I bought in Swan River later. This was an easier form of making hay, rolling it into big thousand pound bales and keeping the hay preserved inside. I didn't use it as it was a favourite of my husband's, so I did all the rest while he baled. One summer I added up all the acres I had cut hay on, both crops, and it added up to more than 2000 acres. Wow! Superwoman was super busy.

But hard and demanding as this was I felt good doing it. I loved to work on the farm, loved our cow-calf operation and loved being an important part of it all. But we never made any money, and the absence of a second income from either Ralph or Brad left a huge gap that someone had to fill. That someone ended up being me. Perfectionist me! Always accommodating me! I sometimes hated myself, as I realized I was carrying most of the load and doing the most worrying. I paid off Ralph's MACC and FCC loans, all $17,000 of it. I bought the newer haying equipment and the three additional parcels of land after we got married. I sold my 53 MG, an antique car, for cash to put into the farms. I sold my nice new convertible, which I'd bought just before our wedding, and got a much cheaper car. I did the books because I knew accounting. I joined and led farm movements to save the family farms in the late 1970s and worked hard to bring up the cattle prices for cow-calf producers. I cashed in bonds, took out my teacher's retirement to invest into the farm, and worked at a regular job with a salary, as well as working at the farm, giving about equal time to both.

What were they doing?

Both men refused to work at an outside job to supplement farm income and cover the farm losses. My salary was the one sure money-making proposition that carried the one that was losing and took care of the three of us, giving us a reasonable living. I carried the cow-calf operation, while my husband and father-in-law got a free ride, doing things when they *felt* like it, treating farming like a hobby. This to me was highly unfair, and I started feeling it. I was tired, aching all the time, and drained financially, physically, and mentally.

It was time for a change.

I knew I was Superwoman and could do so much and wear many hats, but did I always have to be the one to save the day? What was wrong with my partners, two healthy, strong, and able men? Were they just lazy or were they leeching off me? Was this because I was letting them?

> *There is a point in one's life when one gets tired of trying to fix things and make everyone happy. Was I beginning to realize that I didn't need certain people and the bullshit they were bringing into my life?*

We improved our herd, but the cattle prices had dropped dramatically and were below the cost of production, so this was also a strain on all cow-calf operations. I became a activist and a leader in the Canadian Agriculture Movement, a grassroots movement and spin-off of the American Agriculture Movement, demonstrating against the low prices of farm produce. I set up demonstrations in Winnipeg and went to speak in Ottawa, Calgary, and Minnesota for farmers who were losing so much to the middlemen who controlled farm prices while the governments did nothing to help. The family farm was disappearing rapidly, and we felt the governments should help us through the crisis. We were at the mercy of the stock exchange, which set the prices for the produce. The people at the bottom of this pyramid were at the mercy of the few at the top. Brad went to all the meetings with me. He was a great support, and I felt happy to have him there. I was proud that he was also pleased with my efforts. Then I started to wonder if he felt left out, as I was getting most of the attention as the spokesperson and leader. But he never complained. He seemed to like the attention, and I felt he was proud of me. I truly believed he would be comfortable enough with me to tell me the truth of how he felt. I expected this of him and would have done the same myself.

> *The mask, again. The man behind the mask was not the man I saw in the mask.*

I was proud of our little ranch, proud of the herd, proud of being a farmer as well as a teacher, proud of my role in all of it, even though I never sought the credit. I was happy and felt fulfilled, so I didn't need the credit to feel good about my part in it. I felt I had gotten over the need for the approval of men, as I was getting it through my husband and father-in-law, men who never put me down or complained to me. Their approval was what I felt in their love for me.

I was very much a liberalist for the rights of women. Woman could be farmers too. Farming was one of the last occupations to recognize and accept the important role of women. My partners accepted me and let me do what I wanted or needed to do. For me to be accepted as a farm leader, the men in several farm organizations had to think of me as "one of the boys," which always annoyed me. No, I was not the secretary tagging along with the farm leaders! I was one of the leaders! One time when I was in Calgary to meet with the federal Minister of Agriculture, Eugene Whelan, and other high-profile officials, I was asked if I was Karen West, the farm reporter. I was flattered and insulted at the same time, flattered because I respected her as a high-ranking farm reporter and insulted that I wasn't thought of as a farm leader just because I was a woman! The move for women's equality still had a long way to go!

The highlight of that meeting with the federal cabinet minister had to be when I came through the gates at the Calgary airport and was able to recognize Eugene Whelan and Prime Minister Pierre Trudeau walking into the airport at the same time. They had come in a private government jet with all their security guards surrounding them. I just wanted to run up and shake the Honourable Trudeau's hand, but the thought of being arrested stopped me, as I had important things to do in Calgary. My focus wasn't just on meeting with the Minister of Agriculture regarding farm losses that were wiping out family farms on the prairies but on the twenty-minute speech I had ready for the farm rally planned under the Saddle Dome. I was a leader. I had a message. I was Super Farmer, and I was a woman! Hear me roar!

When I arrived at the arena, panic hit me, as gathered together all around me were around five thousand people. The arena was full. I was going to speak to five thousand farm people. This was also being televised nationwide! This was big for a country woman, but Superwoman could handle it. When I got up, the panic subsided. I had a mission, and I had to get my message across. My passion for what I had to say took over. My words came out as though I was someone else, and I was even shocked at what I was saying. When I finished, there was silence, and then the crowd stood up and clapped. A standing ovation for me? A standing ovation for what I had said? I was stunned, and it was over.

A month later, I was featured in Maclean's magazine when the movement, of which I was one of three founders, was the main feature of the edition. I was interviewed and predicted to be a farm leader of the future. Calls even came to my school from news reporters in Manitoba and across Canada, looking for interviews from which I could be quoted. One particular interview amused me. I was having a coffee at Robin's Donuts in Winnipeg when I heard a news commentator from CBC comment on a jail riot in the Saskatchewan federal penitentiary and my name and voice came up, as I was being interviewed and quoted. I wasn't commenting on the jail riot but on the Farm Movement. I laughed at this mistake, which wasn't caught at the time but was corrected later.

This sudden national fame and media attention, with a microphone in my face so often, also shocked me. What was I doing? I was suddenly more than just Superwoman; I was to be a Super Farm Leader in the future. But this never came to be. My personal life was about to fall apart and unravel, and the emerging Super Woman Farmer was to crash and burn. Being a political leader was still a possibility in the distant future, but no longer a farm leader, as I was about to lose the farm and with it the passion for farming.

At home, however, the self-worth was there, and I knew I was still Superwoman and that without me, the farm would collapse. I was the strong one, the backbone of it all, and I knew what and who I was! Or at least I thought I did! It wasn't until the 80s that my self-worth was shaken and my life unraveled day by day as I started finding out the truth that, I was already starting to see.

Being so proud while things were going smoothly, I wanted to give our operation a name. I thought long and hard about it. When all else fails, one can always goes back to the names or the initials. Wasn't that how Canada got its name? C eh? N eh? D eh? That's a joke I heard on the radio! This was using three letters, but this is not really how Canada got its name.

I worked on our initials from our first names for starters. B for Brad, R for Ralph, and M for my legal name. How could I throw these names or initials together? Then I saw it: MBR, eMBeR, and the name of our ranch was born, Ember Ranch. I registered this name, and it stuck for years to come. I was proud of it and the business. Things seemed to be going so well. As a result of the agricultural movement, farm prices started going up again, and I looked forward to just being back home and doing what I enjoyed doing most, owning and operating a ranch.

Things are not always as they seem!

After ten years of bliss, productivity, and happiness, things started to change noticeably, and my life started falling apart as something bigger than I realized became a stalking predator, wearing down his prey day by day as incident after incident happened! I felt something was wrong, and my intuition was making my stomach hurt. Something wasn't right in my world, and I was starting to take note of some of the signs I didn't heed before due to my own ignorance or lack of knowledge.

I was woman. I was invincible, but I was getting tired. Something was not right!

The double life I was living and the double work I was doing was taking its toll. I started getting migraines more frequently than before, and my body was experiencing more pain and stiffness. The migraines had started earlier when I was teaching in Moose Lake, but now were becoming habitual. The pain in different parts of my body became unbearable, and the mental stress was also becoming too much. Depression set in with mood swings from highs to lows. I saw many doctors and specialists but didn't get any acceptable answers for the cause of my severe migraines. I thought there was something seriously wrong with me but figured that it was due to too much heavy work and too many financial worries. I wanted and needed to take a year off teaching to recover. I mentioned quitting my job for at least a year to Brad, and to my surprise, his face flushed red with anger. "Who's going to pay the bills then?" he asked.

I said to him, "Maybe you can get a job for a year!"

His indignant reply was, "Who me? I'm a farmer; I can't get a job!"

I didn't wish to reply with what I was thinking, as I knew it was no use with that kind of attitude. That day, I saw a different person in the man I'd married--I was starting to see the man behind the mask!

Lady, you are finally getting a glimpse of what is behind the mask, something you should have seen a long time ago. You were so blind!

I started to do strange things that I would never have done before. I began reacting to things being done to me and started questioning my life, my relationship, and the man I'd married. For ten years, I was naive, in love, and perhaps didn't want to see what I didn't want to believe. But I was maturing, and thus, this Superwoman was no longer feeling so Super Confident and sure of herself.

I started testing things.

Chapter 15: Reactions and Testing

When in the box, one doesn't see outside of the box.

After ten years of this, my first test was the hay bale test. It started out as accidental but then became a planned strategy to test out my partners. On my way to the farm to stack some square bales of fresh hay, I accidentally dropped two bales off the back of the truck and onto the road to the farmhouse. No one could go down that road if the bales weren't picked up except to go around them. Surely one of the two men would pick them up and put them on the stack. This was in the beginning of August. August went by and so did September and then October, and the two bales were still sitting in exactly the same place where I'd dropped them. No effort had even been made to drag them off the road! The tracks went around the left and the right, but the bales were still there! In the middle of the road!

This told me something I was already beginning to suspect. These two men were lazy and only did things when and if they felt like it. There was no "making hay when the sun was shining," as my father had always done and taught me to do. It was more like "make hay if and when you feel like it." They didn't care about the cow-calf ranch. It was a ranch in name only, and it was an excuse for the men not to have to get a job. They expected me to do all of this, and because I did it, they were okay with dumping the load on me! As Brad always said, **"there is a sucker born every day, and one should take advantage of this."** I guess I was one of these fools, or "suckers." Why should they not take advantage of this? I had been happy being the fool! I was no longer Superwoman; I was Super Fool! This hurt my pride and hurt me as I began to wonder where all of this was going to go. I wondered what they really did all day when I as teaching 50 kilometers from home. It wasn't long before I would find out.

Then, the second test

Brad bought a truck that had been sitting at the side of the road. We saw it when we made a road trip to visit my mother and father. He wanted us to buy this truck. It came out of my teaching money account, not the joint farm account and therefore the truck was registered in my name. I didn't use it, as I had an old wreck of a station wagon to drive. He already had a nice truck to use. When it had to be registered again, I mentioned to Brad I was going to do it, just to see what he would say. He grabbed me and wrestled me to the ground, the registration paper flying into the snow. He then grabbed it and took off to register the truck in his name! I thought, *what's the big deal?* But it showed greed in him and warned me of things to come. I wasn't to be disappointed; they did come.

My mind went back in time to try to figure out when all of this started. I had to go back ten years. Sometimes we have to look into the past to find what motivates people to do the things they do in the present. Brad had quit his surveying job a year after he married me, as he said he was going to be a farmer. I thought I'd be able to quit my job, too, but then who would bring home the bacon and finish our house or buy the equipment needed for the farm? Who would pay the bills? Neither Brad nor his father had any money, only debts! I kept working at my teaching job and at the ranch. I loved working at the ranch, as it was a change from dealing with high school students in my business and art classes at Powerview High School. It was good exercise as well. Cattle, horses, and dogs were my favourite domesticated animals. I enjoyed being surrounded by nature in the pristine area where I lived. I loved working on the swather, the haybind, and the baler, and I enjoyed putting up hay. It always smelled so good. Sometimes I worked too hard and then couldn't walk for a while, but that was all natural and normal until the pain worsened. The pains came from too much straining of my muscles, which came from too much work! I had to slow down!

Then the migraines I'd been experiencing for a few years grew more frequent. They hit with a fury and a vengeance, making me bedridden and unable to move until I could get rid of them. My head hurt so much, and I felt so nauseated. I usually had a stomach of steel, or so I thought, and migraines were the only thing that could make me vomit. Nausea and diarrhea at the same time! My head and my butt kept taking turns at the toilet. These migraines would build up into what I called migraine marathons. I was prescribed Fiornal and Codeine, which some people told me were barbiturates. I didn't know, as I wasn't one of the flower children of the 60s. I never smoked, drank, or took illegal drugs other that what I was prescribed. Working up north, in the 60s, I was far removed from the scenes that were so obvious in the bigger cities. These medications worked and allowed me to go to work, but they were Band-Aid's to a problem I was still unaware of. At times when they'd hang on and not go away, I'd have to go to emergency, where they give me an injection. I never asked what was in the needles, and when I was told at one of my visits to a doctor, that they were morphine, I was shocked and didn't want them anymore. Later, these prescriptions were changed to 222s with codeine, and Demerol shots when needed, as the pain specialist at the Health Sciences Center, Dr. Krukshank, said I was too young to take morphine or any barbiturates.

These worked just as well, and my worry about taking such addictive drugs was appeased for the time being; however, I still wanted to know why I was getting the migraines, but no one could tell me. I even had a CT scan, which revealed nothing. I also wanted to know why I wasn't conceiving children. I had a mystery disease that no one could figure out at that time, and so it was not given a name, as it still was not understood.

I was now living in constant pain. Life had become a struggle, but I had to live with it. Dr. Krukshank, the pain specialist, told me that I'd be in pain for the rest of my life, so I should get used to it. He told me I had to mentally get through what he called the "barrier of pain." This meant to psych myself into not feeling the pain. I worked on this, and in time I didn't feel the pain, but I went a little too far. I once put my hand on the stove burner to see if it was hot, and I burned my fingers but felt no pain. This shocked me and made me realize I needed to back up a little with the psyching out bit. I needed to feel pain so I would know I was doing something to cause it. In time, I found a balance, and pain became my buddy. I was told I had osteoarthritis, so I named this pain, Art! Art was my first buddy, and Henry, the hiatal hernia, was next on the list. I could deal with pain when I could see the humour in it. The mystery disease ended up being Freddy, but this would not be discovered until many years later. I realized later that all my pains had male names! Did this mean anything? That men could be a pain? Even though I was often depressed or anxious, I could still laugh at things, as I had learned to do, from my father.

I never stopped looking for answer at pain clinics, at the Pam Am Clinic in Winnipeg, at chiropractors' offices, at neurologists' offices, and at pain specialists' offices. Everything came up empty, and most of the time I was told there was nothing wrong with me. I was made to feel like a hypochondriac seeking attention. That ticked me off, as I knew I wasn't making it up. If could psych myself out of feeling pain then the pain was actually far greater than I could feel. After a while, I began to think of myself as a hypochondriac. How easily we can be indoctrinated! When bombarded with the same information over and over.

Why was I also suffering such pain in my hip, legs, and the rest of my body? At first, I thought it was the hard work, but when this persisted all winter long as well, I knew there was something very wrong with me. I started to believe that I had a mystery disease, and a mystery it would remain for a long time. I was in severe pain, had debilitating migraines, and then my stomach started reacting as well. There was nothing I could do, as I didn't know what to do! I had to learn to tolerate pain. Life became an everyday struggle, but I couldn't let it get me down. I trained my mind to think of other things and kept myself busy all the time. I just wanted to be Super Normal! I wanted to be happy.

I did well! I could focus on other things and forget the pain.

I was getting used to this illness and could handle it, as I was still so happy with my life, my husband, and our ranch. I did the book work and sought out breeding stock. Within ten years, we had one of the best herds in the country, according to farm journals. We were the promising new farmers of the future; we were popular, loved, and so happy. Having little money was no problem, as money wasn't important, but paying off bills was. I liked to take care of business and wanted us to be out of debt and able to plan a future. We were finally there after ten years of marriage! We'd soon be able to relax a little, and I could seriously think of having children. We could do this now; we were out of the fog!

But this was all an illusion, and bad things were starting to happen. The signs were to become reality.

When I was ready to have children, I still couldn't conceive, in spite of seeking medical advice and undergoing many tests. This concerned me. I finally was prepared to try one more thing that would cost me but I was prepared to pay the price. It was to try In Vitro Fertilization at a St. Boniface clinic. I so wanted children, even though my doctor advised me to adopt.

Life was still good, and we were still very happy and in love, I thought. One teacher at school told me that we looked like a couple who would stay together for life, and I felt the same. I had put aside the thought of being used, and the partnership as being unfair, because I did not wish to think about it.

Dark night!
No air!
Stark naked!
People staring at me!
Then alone!
All alone!
I was alone

This dream came back to me. I woke up feeling sick to my stomach and so incredibly sad. But I wasn't alone; he was there right beside me in our bed. I put my arms around him and felt him stir. It was wonderful; I felt happy again. Then I fell asleep feeling warm, loved, and so content, a far cry from being alone. He was there! Why was I having these horrible dreams? Who was trying to reach me through signs? What was I supposed to find out?

Sometimes, I thought back to Teachers' College and the nice man I dated who'd asked me to consider marrying him. I felt badly at times when I looked at his grad picture, which I cherished, and wondered how much I had hurt him. I also wondered where he was and what had happened to him, and I wished I could see him and tell him I was sorry. But why was I even thinking of him when I had Brad? Time would tell; time would tell!

Yes, this marriage was predestined to last forever, just as the vow we had taken, "'til death us do part." I secretly hoped I would die before him, as I couldn't stand to lose him. I loved him so much. I sometimes thought of Joe and hoped he was as happily married as I was. I had done the right thing; I had chosen the right man, I thought. My destiny was sealed. We could have children through In Vitro Fertilization when I had enough money saved up for it, or we could adopt. My future was carved in stone with the words, wonderful, wonderful, and wonderful scripted on the rock! We had good friends who were couples like ourselves, had the same interests, and would also be our friends forever. Life was good.

Sometimes we want to believe the illusions because reality is too hard to take.

However, the gods determined a different destiny for me, one I would never have expected at that time. Everything was about to change after the first ten years. The heaven I was in turned to the ugliest, most twisted and evil hell one could ever imagine. I asked myself many times what I had done in my *last life* to deserve this, as I had done nothing in the present one to deserve such horrible punishment and abuse! Thoughts of reincarnation popped into my head. Was it possible to have lived as another person or creature in the past? To have done things then, that this life would have to counterbalance? Wrongs to be righted, or good to be rewarded? I read something in an astrology paper that said I'd had a wicked neighbour in my last life, and that was the reason for my suffering in this life. *Darn, rotten neighbour*, I thought, and I wished I could have bashed him in the head. But that was only a thought. I could never be violent.

Chapter 16: The Dreams

Night without air!
A pillow over my head!
No air!
I can't breathe!
Scream!
No one will hear!
I was alone!
Completely
Alone!

The dreams were becoming more frequent now, and the four things meshed into one: a pillow over my head, death, shame, and being alone. I would be in the middle of a small field with trees around it, sitting by myself with people sitting or standing all around me, gawking at me. I'd look at myself and see that I was stark naked with nothing to cover myself with, and the people would all be staring at me. I'd be so embarrassed, and then I'd wake up. Other times I dreamt of being at the bottom of a grave and having dirt thrown on me. When having these recurring dreams, I would wake up gasping for air. What did it mean? Even though he was still there beside me, warm as ever, there was something to these dreams, I was beginning to think. Perhaps a message from the subconscious? Was this a premonition of what was to come? Were our brains designed to foretell the future? There was still so much to be learned about this part of our body, the human brain, which controls all and is still such a mystery to us. The brain is capable of more than we can possibly imagine. We still have a lot to learn about mental health.

I became worried and wanted to hurry and have children in case our childlessness became a reason for him to leave me, so I would find myself alone. I tried so hard. I did the thermometer thing and then wore a beautiful negligee and had a glass of wine before making love. I was ready to conceive, but nothing worked, and it wasn't for lack of trying.

Something was wrong; I could sense it. Why the dreams? Was I about to be alone soon? Was I about to die? I watched the movie *Love Story*, and it so paralleled my life. The woman couldn't conceive, and during the tests they found out she had cancer. She died in the end. Did I have cancer? What really shocked me in this story was watching the young couple happily driving a 1953 MG convertible. It was like the one I had, and we often drove it for fun and laughter. Was this the preview of what my life would be like? Unlike the man in *Love Story*, would my husband leave me if he found out I had cancer? Not all men can take this … could mine? So many horrible thoughts went through my head, but I was wrong in all respects. But I wasn't wrong to think I had something to worry about, I did! It would be far worse than being left alone …far worse. It was the beginning and cause of what would come down on me later: Post-Traumatic Stress. But this was only another symptom of something far broader in scope and worse than PTSD, the mystery disease that no one could identify at that time.[12]

I was becoming a victim in more ways than one, a victim to the man I married, and a victim to the effects of what he was doing to me that would escalate in the early 80's, the years I would call five years of hell. I felt helpless and alone, as there was no one I could or would talk to. I was also imprisoned in my thoughts, but I was too naive, too ignorant to know what this meant. These were things no one had ever taught me, nothing I had read about. I was too ashamed to ask. It was subtle and took years to happen, and to me it seemed normal until things started getting weird and bizarre, because of the "make crazy" things others do to us until we start to think we're going insane and become the scapegoats for the wrong doing of others. When people with problems are in denial, they won't accept ownership for their problems, especially when they can find others to "transfer" them to, or blame for these problems. This takes them off the hook. But I knew none of this then.

---

12   See Appendix for Post-traumatic Stress Disorder

Chapter 17: The Family That Never Was!

For over ten years, our marriage had seemed too perfect. It was too perfect! We did everything together as a team and seemed so in love. Even though I found the men lax when farming, other things compensated for it. We worked at the farm and took many trips, both business and for fun. We didn't have a lot of money, but that didn't matter, as each vacation could be a campout for as cheap as we could manage, but still a lot of fun. So many places to see together! We went to Corpus Christi, Mexico, Thunder Bay, Vernon, and Victoria. We slept in the station wagon when we didn't have relatives or friends to bunk with.

Then it happened! A small miracle! A wonderful boy came to us, a three-year old by the name of Ricky. It was like a gift from heaven and would solidify our union. We would be a family. This seemed to be the answer to our strained marriage. He was so sweet and needed a home. He'd been abandoned by his parents and was being taken care of by his grandfather, who asked us if we'd take him. Ricky was in the hands of Children's Aid, and we would receive money for looking after him. In time, we could apply to adopt. It was like a miracle that was meant to happen, I thought at the time. Good things come in small packages, and this small package was a three-year old boy by the name of Ricky!

This little gift fit in like our very own. People even remarked about how he looked like us: bright eyes, loving, and so sweet! To keep him company, we put in for the adoption of another child with Child and Family Services. I applied to adopt a three-year old girl, was accepted and just had to take an orientation course. We also put in for Ricky's adoption. Then one day the social worker came to take Ricky to spend the weekend with his father, she said. The boy cried his little heart out as he was leaving, but I assured him, it would only be for three sleeps. I watched him shoot the social worker in the eye with a water pistol when she bent over to talk to him in private. I was shocked at that. Did he know what was going to happen? Do children know these things by intuition? Or was this fear that he was going to lose me if he left with the social worker?

He was right to have this fear.

He never came back. I called CFS but was told, "Didn't you know? We were taking him away for good." At the time, I couldn't understand why. My heart was breaking. Little did I think at that time that having a child was cutting into something far more important to my husband than the family I thought he wanted? It was a good thing I didn't know, or I might have done something drastic. I fought with CFS to change their mind and give him back. When I realized that it wasn't going to happen, I mourned Ricky's absence every time I looked at his toys and clothes still in the closet.

Then CFS phoned to let us know we were to have an orientation meeting for the girl. My husband answered and told them we were having marital problems, and this wasn't a good time.

Marital problems? That finally put things into context and into words, but reality can sound so cruel. Things hadn't been as good as usual for a while, but marital problems? That seemed a little extreme; I could see nothing so drastic that couldn't be fixed with a little work by both of us. I started to wonder what made him think we had marital problems, although I could feel some of the strain. It seemed as though he wanted this. But again, I thought it would never happen, that we would work things out, and it was just a difficult time with losing Ricky. It was far worse, than that.

Then something strange happened. Sometimes things happen we just can't explain or get our minds around and we like to think that nothing foul could happen in the small in our small town. But there was something very foul! I just couldn't see it at the time.

Chapter 18: The Mysterious Incident

It was the middle of the next spring after Ricky had left that a strange thing happened. I was still missing him, but our love life seemed to have improved, and I thought that perhaps Brad didn't want other people's children but wanted our own instead. I remembered the In Vitro Fertilization and decided to get it if it would save our marriage.

We were about ready to start seeding oats at the parcel of land by our residence, which was six kilometers from our farm and farm house. We were going to seed a cover crop of oats mixed with pasture seed. The pasture seedlings are fragile the first year, so a cover crop of oats is protective of the little seedlings. We had our best friends visiting us, who were also farmers, the Koziers. I had made coffee for us, and we were sitting around the table shooting the bull, as we called it. Suddenly, Brad got up and said he had to go to the farm to get the combination of the seed drill for the oats we wanted to plant. I was a little surprised at this, as one doesn't get up and leave when we have guests! It was rude, and he wasn't usually a rude person. He took off around four o'clock. The Koziers stayed awhile and then left, and I was alone in the house.

I got a call from Brad at around 6:00 p.m. He asked me to go to the farm and take his father to the hospital, as he had been injured. I asked myself, why can't Brad take him? The farm is only ten minutes from the Pinawa hospital, and he has the truck? But then I thought he must need me to help get Ralph into the vehicle. I went to the farm to find Ralph staggering outside and ready to go to the hospital. He had suffered a severe blow to top back of his head and second one to his shoulder. Brad didn't know what had happened to him; he said he just found him that way.

But he had left two hours ago, I thought to myself. Why call this late?

I took Ralph and Brad to the hospital where Ralph was admitted. The doctor asked us if he'd been drinking. I thought that was a bit strange, but then again, Ralph was staggering. We told him that Ralph didn't drink. On the way home, Brad and I talked about what could have happened, as apparently Ralph had been cutting a few small poplars at the farm. He lived near Old Pinawa Dam in the small farm house he'd repaired after a fire. He lived there alone. He always locked the door, even when he went to sit in the outdoor toilet. He was very cautious.

I kept thinking about what possibly could have happened to him. Brad told me he'd found his father lying on the couch when he got there. Ralph couldn't tell us what had happened, so I thought it was likely a tree that had hit him. The next day, I went by the farm on my way to the hospital to see Ralph. I went alone, and on my way I could see where Ralph had been cutting trees, but they were only saplings. There was no way they could have been that heavy to cause such a serious concussion. It all seemed very strange to me.

Ralph didn't recognize me at first, when I went to visit him in the hospital, the next day. The doctor said he'd suffered a serious concussion and would be staying in the hospital for a while. Brad refused to go with me, which I also found strange. On another day I went to the hospital and he was gone! The doctor told me he'd been transferred to a Winnipeg hospital for further tests, but he wouldn't tell me why. He was gone for a month, and when he got back, I could see the fear in his eyes. He told me someone had hit him from behind and asked why we hadn't gone to the police. I wondered why he hadn't gone to the police. I knew of nothing that could substantiate that he'd been the victim of foul play. Everything seemed too weird.

But he kept repeating that someone had hit him on the head. I wasn't sure what to believe anymore. When I spoke to friends, the Rosentrators, they told me that Brad had told them he found his father on the floor when he got to the farm on the night he was injured. That was not what I'd been told. What was with this discrepancy? Then I started to tell myself that Ralph had suffered a stroke and had been injured by a fall, but it didn't make sense, as this was a blow to the top of his head and shoulder. It seemed very suspicious. Then I started believing that someone had indeed hit him on the head. But who would do such a horrible thing, and why? Ralph was well liked in the town. He was dirt poor as far as having ready cash, but he owned a lot of property, property I had paid down the debts on, thinking Brad had a stake in them. He had nothing worth stealing in the house, and the house was always locked up tight when he wasn't there, so it wasn't likely someone was hiding in the house before he got home. But one person had a key who could have gotten in ahead of Ralph and lay in wait for him. And that person was my husband, his son.

And the only one who might have a motive ... a very good one! A selfish one!

Could it have been him? Is that why he told different stories, because he was making them up and had forgotten what he'd told people? That's the biggest problem with making up lies, it's easy to forget the first story, and so different stories come out of it. When it's the truth, there's only one story.

I'd always wondered why these two men were verbally abusive to each other. I'd never witnessed such language before but I was aware of love/hate relationships and thought that perhaps this was one of them. I felt that my husband was often quite cruel to his father--unnecessarily cruel--but the father could also be cruel in reply. I was ashamed of my thinking, as Brad was such a gentle, mild man. He couldn't possibly have done it, and if he had, I would think his father would suspect him and go to the RCMP. I was still confused and still thought my stroke theory was the correct one.

We don't want to believe what could be the truth when we don't wish for our illusions to be destroyed. Who knows what really goes on in secrecy or behind closed doors?

And then in fall 1982, his father said he was leaving for good! He was going to BC and would stay there with his sister and her husband. I gathered he was afraid that whoever hit him would come back to finish the job. He couldn't stay at the farmhouse alone anymore because of this fear. I was sad, as I had come to love the old man. He had character. He was a good-looking man, gentle, and independent. I often cooked for the three of us, as he didn't make much for meals for himself. I cleaned up his house, as he wasn't much of a housekeeper either. I tried to give the farmhouse the woman's touch, and make him feel good living in it. He had lived off and on with a woman he'd gotten involved with after the loss of Brad's mother when Brad was quite young, so he also had two stepchildren, Brad's stepsister and stepbrother, who were around the same age as Brad.

Ralph came to our place a lot for meals, and my routine became, pick up hay with the men, come to the house to whip up a meal for the three of us, do dishes while the men have a nap after dinner, and then go back on the field with them to pick up hay again. I so enjoyed working with them and saw it was an opportunity to bond, which didn't happen too often after our first years of marriage. This amount of work I was doing wasn't always fair, but I was okay with it as after all, I could do more than the ordinary mortal on this earth. I could play many roles; I could do twice as much as they could! I was Superwoman! Don't ever forget who you are, the persona you have invented! I told myself.

I said I was Superwoman, and I was determined to stay in that role: a teacher, an accountant, an artist, a farmer, a housewife, a cook, a leader for farm movements, an environmentalist, a political activist, and a motivational speaker! No grass growing under my feet, and no dull moments for me! I would continue to be everything to everybody, needed and loved, and this gave me a feeling of self-worth. It built up my ego and made me feel proud and happy to be who I thought I was. Superwoman to the max! God, I was good ... or so I thought to myself.

We bought out Ralph's share of the cattle, before he left to go to BC for good! But something interesting happened just before he left that fall. Brad had him and I sign papers for land transfers. As I was the wife, I had marital (homestead) rights. I didn't know that Brad previously didn't have a title for the land we were living on, or any of the farms we were farming. The only ones he had title on were the ones I'd bought, as I had the bill of sale made to us jointly and registered it with Land Titles as such. I just assumed he had title for the other parcels of land, jointly with his father, as he talked as though he had. I was too busy doing everything else to look into this, and I was the woman of trust, trust and faith in her man! After all, he was my husband, and this meant trusting him! Before this transaction took place, Brad told me I had to sign off, even though the land wasn't being transferred in both of our names, as this wasn't necessary. He told me that in the event we got divorced (but of course, we never would, he said), I was still entitled to half of everything, since I was his wife. I was satisfied with this, and I believed him. I knew nothing of the law, but I felt he wouldn't cheat me or cheat on me ever! And I still believed in the "til death do us part" crap, which meant to love and honor each other until death … not wanting to think that death could be arranged by one of us to part us. I signed as I had to, as I was told to. No sweat. And then we said goodbye to Ralph. I did not realize that having the farms in his name only, could be a problem if we ever got divorced. And now, his step brother and step sister would have no claim on them, either.

You are a Super Fool … too trusting! You have just been deceived! Now the three farms were in Brad's name, and the only ones in his name and my name jointly were the three parcels of land I had bought with my teaching money! I was told by my dear friend, Alvina, to get them in both of our names, and to this day I thank her for her words of wisdom. She was much less trusting than I was! Maybe she had reason to be, as she'd known both Ralph and Brad much longer than I had! Our house was on land his father signed over, also in Brad's name only. Potential trouble!

Then another incident happened. To this day, I still wonder how I could have been so blind, foolish, naive, and trusting! What a fool I was! Not a Super Woman any longer, but a too trusting and blind, a Super Fool!

I signed a cheque to Ralph, for $15,000 from our business account, to buy out his share of the cattle. Did Ralph ever get to keep this money, or did Brad wheedle this out of his father as well. Later, I made out a cheque for $1000 as a wedding gift to his father when he married a woman in BC. This money ended up in a bank account in Brad's name in Vernon, BC. I got to see the bankbook, which Maggie, Ralph's new wife, showed me. Who got the $15,000 for Rolf's cattle in the end? I started to wonder. At that time, nothing seemed to be wrong and yet things did not seem to be right, either. The $15,000 was made out to Ralph, and I expected Ralph would get it. I didn't know how afraid this man was of his own son, and that he'd been threatened.

Ralph never came back to stay, but later that fall, after he'd left, I found something very interesting. It was my first clue that I had a guardian angel point me into the right direction to discover something I wasn't supposed to see! Something done behind my back, in secrecy, led me to see the two-faced character of the man behind the mask. For the first time, I started to believe, I was the victim of lies and deceit!

I had picked up a sheet of paper from a writing block and could easily see the imprint of what was written on the preceding page that had been torn off. I was curious, as Brad wasn't a letter writer, and this was definitely his handwriting. He only wrote beautiful love letters to me, when we were courting, and hadn't written any letters since, that I knew of. The content was shocking to me. I rubbed over the paper with pencil shading and the message came out clearly. It was a letter he had written to his father, who was now living in BC. It said: "She is never happy with anything I do. I'm thinking of getting rid of her." But he didn't explain how. This indicated to me that he was tired of our relationship and wanted out of it. It shocked me, as what he said about me wasn't true. I had never spoken badly of him, so why was he speaking badly of me? Was he planning something against me? Was this an attempt to turn his father against me with his lies?

Sometimes things are so strange, we don't need to go looking for the truth, as it will find us. This was one of those cases. What were the chances of me finding the imprint of his letter in the first place? But I did. It was definitely a sign that someone greater than myself had pointed out to me. Now I could finally read a sign that was so obvious in this letter. He wanted to get rid of me! Why? For greed? All of the six parcels of land were now in his name, with only three in both names. So if he got rid of me, he would have them all.

Chapter 19: Lies and Deceit!

My migraines never stopped, nor did my pain. I had bought three cows, and brought them to where we lived on River Road, so I could milk them. I drank a lot of milk, as this was the only thing that relieved the burning in my stomach. I was tired of running to one specialist after another to find out what was wrong with me, and there seemed to be so many things. There was only one disease that incorporated all of these symptoms but it was still a mystery disease.

These are all parts of the disease you have, lady, and do not know anything about!

Then a new dream came, and this one was horrifying to me, a person who loved walking, exploring, and hiking. While walking, my legs froze up on me, and I couldn't walk anymore. I couldn't take a step forward, as the ability to move my legs, was gone. But these were only dreams. I had no clue what they meant, but there was a similar theme running through them. They were all the "end of the road" as I knew it. My life was ending, and I could go no further in my dreams, there was no rescue evident, no saving grace, no way out. The end was coming, scary! But the end of what? My life? My relationship? My health?

Most dreams with problems end up with a solution ... unless there is none!

I was always a problem-solver when young, and as a teacher we learned problem-solving as well. Every problem has solutions, I learned. If option A was tried and did not work, we could go to option B. I was good at this and prided myself in my ability to solve problems effectively. But these dreams offered no solution, and I could see no solution, as I didn't know what the dreams were about or what the problem really was. I found it frustrating, as the worst thing in the world for me is "not knowing" the truth. When one knows the truth, they can deal with it. But how does one deal with the unknown, with the cover ups, with the secrets when we have no ideas of what we need to deal with? These dreams were the unknown, they were elusive, yet the message was strong: the end of something was coming, and they were warning me to be prepared for something horrible. The frequency and intensity of the dreams told me it would happen soon, and there was no solution! I even went to a sand reader and made some drawings in the sand. The reader refused to read them, gave me my money back, and told me my future was so terrible, she didn't want to read it! Wow! How could she possibly know this from the circle I drew in the sand? I couldn't tell anyone, not even my husband, as I really did not know what to say.

My sleepy little tourist town had some dark secrets. Every little town has it dark side, undercurrents of evil that can't be seen until you find yourself floundering in them. I loved my town; it was beautiful and so charismatic. When I first got there, I felt like I was going back in time, coming from a modern Northern community to a rustic redneck town with old buildings like the Lakeview and the old pharmacy. When I first went to a pub with Brad I was surprised at the profane language in the booth next to us. It was filled with rednecks, or some might call them hillbillies. The countryside was different; it had been settled by people from Scandinavia: Norwegians, Finns, Swedes, and Latvians. All wonderful people! But there were a number of suspicious happenings that were called suicides but smelled like murder to me. It sometimes gave me eerie feelings like there were ghosts walking about in the darkness that disappeared into the night. What were this town's secrets? Would the truth ever be found, or would it be as elusive as these ghosts of the night? Who really knows what happens behind closed doors, what love triangles there are, what vows are fatally broken? What dreams are crushed forever! But on the other hand, all seemed so innocent. People were friendly, and we got to associate with other farmers and some elderly couples who were hospitable and helpful. I soon felt at home in this rustic town on the edge of the Canadian Shield and nestled beside the Winnipeg River.

I had bought some horses to add to our ranch. It started with one horse, then two, and then a purebred Arabian stallion, which was the start of my riding stable that I would have for the next twenty years. I witnessed the birth of many foals sired by this beautiful white stallion. Training came easy for me, as I had joined the 4-H horse and calf club as a leader. This taught me much about horses, and training them seemed like a gift to me, a gift that was very therapeutic at a time of marital stress. I participated in many riding workshops, read up on horses, and soon became a trainer of horses and children with horses. I quit the leadership role of the horse and calf club, as I wanted to work with children and horses rather than deal with the paperwork and administration of the 4-H clubs. I took lessons in judging and later entered shows with my horses. This turned out to be my support and escape when my marriage fell to pieces and sinister plots were being conceived behind my back.

We became parents again. The autumn that Ralph left was such an eventful year! It was a turn in the tide of tension. We became foster parents to a teenage daughter, which was quite a change from Ricky, a three-year old boy! I had put aside the imprint on the letter, put the dark dreams on a back burner, and felt that all was well again, and we could be good parents to a messed up sixteen-year-old.

> ***You are so blind, lady. Wake up and smell the coffee!***
> ***You may think this is God's plan for you, but there is a***
> ***demon at work here! Things are not always what they seem!***
> ***Have you forgotten your father's words of wisdom?***

I'd been asked to take in Laurel, who was originally from a farm and loved horses. She had some serious psychological issues and had been placed in an institution by her parents. So we went from a three-year-old to a very curvy, sexy sixteen year-old who had the smile and the hairdo of Farrah Fawcett ... when she did smile. She didn't smile often. The blue eyes were striking! She could have been my daughter, as I also had blue eyes, but mine weren't as striking. Often in public, people thought we were sisters. I liked that, as it was very complimentary to be told that I still looked young enough to be her sister when I was old enough to be her mother. I was in my late-thirties.

I worked hard on her, to get her to talk and to bring her back to living a normal life. She seemed depressed and very reserved. In time, she started to talk. She loved to work with my horses and started coming around. My husband was also good with her, but it seemed he was a little too good; not that I felt I needed to compete with her for his attention. He was devoting more and more time to her, and less and less to me. Sometimes I had funny feelings about this and told myself I was just being jealous. I was so wrong and it was my gut that was so right. We need to listen to our gut.

Half a year later, an incident occurred that would add to the trauma of my life and to the emotional stress that fed the disease that was still a mystery to me, a disease that was progressive. Things would build up to a point where an explosion of sorts had to happen. It would also become the trigger device for future PTSD. This was the making of future nightmares, future pain, future mental stress, and memories that would not leave my head! Ever!

They say our keenest and most realistic memories are not of our happiest moments but the moments of our worst anguish.

It was in the middle of January 1983, a very cold, icy night. My husband and I always went to dances together and had a lot of fun. Both of us, being excellent dancers, could make the bystanders look on with envy and awe as we whirled around the dance floor to polkas, waltzes, and schottisches. The night at a social always went by too quickly. They were happy times.

We were good dancers and made good partners on the dance floor.

The little subtle things that had been happening in our home were beginning to affect me. I was grouchy and felt anxiety. We had bought tickets to a social to be held at our favourite place to dance and where a lot of our friends would be, the Great Falls Hall. I always looked forward to these dances, but that night I felt sick to my stomach. Was I anxious or what? Depressed like my mother? I mentioned that I didn't feel well, hoping my husband would try to convince, or even beg me to go, as I was already feeling left out in my own home. It didn't happen. What did happen was a flippant "Okay, I'll take Laurel instead." I was shocked that he would want to take her and sound so happy about me not going! She didn't even know how to dance our old-fashioned dances, but she loved to drink. We were never drinkers, just dancers. I stayed at home and cried myself to sleep. But this sleep didn't last. When he left, he did say something to make me feel a little better: "Since you're not going, we're just going to make an appearance and will be home by twelve." I woke up at twelve, but no one had come home. One o'clock and still they hadn't come home. The minutes ticked by so slowly. I got up and paced the floor, worried that the icy road and drink combination might have led to a fatal accident.

At two o'clock I couldn't stand it anymore; I visualized a car overturned with two bodies in the ditch and no one going by at two in the morning to spot them. I drove to the hall and found nothing. Where could they be? I drove back home, and still no one had shown up. It was getting close to three, and the dance hall always closed at 1:00 p.m. It was a fifteen minute ride home! I couldn't stand the waiting any longer, so I needed something to do. It was close to calving time and very cold, so I drove to the farm to see if any calves might be arriving that night.

At three o'clock in the morning, I got into the old '56 Chevy and drove off. As I headed up the driveway and got close to the farmhouse, my car lights picked up the smoke coming from the chimney. This house, where his father had lived, was now empty in winter, and to heat it a fire had to be started in a wood stove. Why was the fire on? I got closer and saw his truck. I felt my heart lurch right down into the pit of my stomach! What was my husband doing with our foster daughter at the farmhouse at three in the morning, with a cozy fire and a bed in there? They must have seen my lights coming down the long driveway and quickly came out, fully clothed but looking disheveled. Laurel turned white as a sheet, and I just whipped around, got into my car, and headed back home. I remember driving a hundred miles an hour in an old car on very icy roads, seeing the rocks on the side and not caring if I crashed into them and died.

If there ever was something that could have triggered a lifetime of post-traumatic stress, that was the moment. I trusted my husband and never dreamt he would cheat on me, and with our foster daughter on top of it all. Sick, sick, sick! I thought, this man was sick, our relationship was sick, this foster daughter was sick, and I was sick! I got home, packed my bags, and was ready to leave just as they arrived. The first thing he said to me was "It's not what you think!" I really didn't know what to think, as it was all so hurtful to me. My head ached, my stomach ached, and my heart ached, I was so traumatized at the time. I was not Superwoman anymore; I was a Super Zombie. The pain numbed me, but I could still feel the lump in my stomach.

Yeah, they all say that, but don't believe them. "It's not what you think!" It was three in the morning. What was he doing there with her? You know what he would be doing!

Not once did he mention that he had been there to check the calves; if he had, then he would have been more believable. But he didn't. He hadn't thought it out too well, I thought to myself. But why would he even think I would go to the farm at three in the morning? Did I get there before or after they rolled around on the bed? I'm guessing after, as they were fully dressed and ready to leave for home by then! They had to have been there for at least two to three hours. She seemed a little drunk. And him? I couldn't tell; I couldn't even let him come close to me. I was sick, sick, and sick that night and just wanted to get out and run away from home, run away from the pain, run away from them. He convinced me to stay, and not knowing where to go at that time of the night, I did stay home. I needed to give myself some time to figure things out. It was just too much of a shell shock! I needed to think! I couldn't think in that environment. I needed to get away … far, far away. But where could I possibly go?

It was hard for me over the next while because I kept thinking about the scene at the farm, especially when living in the same house as the two of them. I was reminded of it every time I saw them. I kept imagining him making love to her, a young sixteen-year-old. I wondered if she would get pregnant. All these thoughts, right or wrong, raced through my head.

What do I do: stay, or leave?

Maybe I was just imagining the whole thing and was just jealous of a young girl with a body that was very attractive to men. The "getting older" syndrome, as I called it. But this made me very ill. I couldn't sleep or eat for seven days. I tried to teach and get through the day until one day I couldn't. I went to the washroom at the school, exhausted, and started to cry and couldn't stop. I had left my class unattended and knew I couldn't go back to it. Luckily, it was a Grade Eleven accounting class, and the students were mature! I started to vomit. The pain in me was like a rock at the bottom of my stomach. I knew I needed help. I got myself together, went to the empty staff room, and phoned a friend who was a doctor at the psychiatric hospital in Selkirk. I told her what I was going through, and she told me to go there right away. A different doctor would see me because she knew me and that would be a conflict of interest.

I let the school office know I was sick and had to go to the hospital. I went to see the doctor and told him I was going crazy, as I'd never felt that way before, and I wanted to be committed. I told him my story, talking and crying for about two hours. He prescribed meds and told me what he thought had happened--a short circuit in my brain caused by trauma. I went to see him every week after that. Brad went once, lied to him, and refused to go again, as there was nothing wrong with him, according to him! I was the crazy one! Little did I know I was playing right into his game plan for me! There was a dark, evil plot being hatched in the brain of someone I loved, someone I trusted, someone I was sleeping with. A plot I couldn't see as possible in any human being I knew.

> **Isn't that the way it usually is? He will never take any responsibility for his actions. Why should he? You make it easy for him, as you feel guilty and think you're in the wrong. You are easy prey for men like him! You are his scapegoat.**

The doctor believed Brad at first but later told me, after seeing me for several sessions, that this man could "fool the devil" himself. He said that I was going through a lot of trauma because of finding Laurel and Brad together at the farm. There was a short circuit in my brain caused by three things lining up just right: my high expectations, my environment, and the traumatic stress of the farm incident. A spouse's cheating can be very traumatic for women, especially when she thinks the other woman is a younger, prettier, and sexier. The medication he gave me would bridge this short circuit in my nerves and make me feel less depressed.

It took a while, but they worked. They gave me highs and lows, but they stabilized me enough so I could sleep and eat again and, most important of all to me, to do my job at school. Meanwhile, I played right into the hands of my husband's master plan for me, as he could tell everyone, "See, I told you she was crazy. She's going to see a shrink, not me, but her! She's the crazy one, just like her mother was." I was even believing I was crazy myself. When I said this to Delores, a good friend of mine who was very knowledgeable about abuse; she told me I wasn't crazy but was being made crazy. Later in life, I understood the "make crazy" things abusers do to their victims. This was also part of the master plan to get rid of me. Plan B: to drive me crazy and drive me into an institution or to suicide. The first option, which I labelled Plan A, was murder, which was far worse. Or was it? What can possibly be worse than mental torture lasting for a long time? Psychological abuse is just as damaging as physical abuse, the former being torture of the mind.

The doctor also said that if he had seen Brad a second time, as he wanted to, he would have seen through my husband. I guess that was why Brad never went back; he was too cunning to get caught in his lies!

Chapter 20: Double Shock, More Trauma!

Winter went and spring came that year. It was three in the morning when the phone rang and woke me up. Brad jumped out of bed to answer it instantly. He spoke softly to whomever it was who had called, and I couldn't hear what he was saying. I thought this was done on purpose, as I was already becoming paranoid. It couldn't be Laurel, as she was sleeping in our basement suite. Then he asked me to come to the phone, as someone wanted to talk to me. This totally caught me off guard. Who would wish to speak to me at that ungodly hour of the morning? After the loss of my eighteen-year-old nephew, these middle-of-the-night calls were *never* good news. In a sense, it wasn't good news, but it was also good in that it woke me up to reality and the truth that up to that point, I was trying to avoid.

"Hello?" I spoke into the phone.

"Hi this is Danielle; I need to see you right away. Can you come over to see me?"

"Now?" I asked

"Right now. I have something important to tell you."

"Okay, I'll get dressed and be over in ten minutes."

"I'll be waiting for you." Danielle was a woman that lived about a kilometer away from us, down River Road. I only knew her as our insurance agent, and heard that Brad had dated her, before me.

I got dressed and drove five minutes to her place, in total numbness. My gut had a knot in it, and I felt shaky, as my body anticipated what I was about to hear after my suspicions of what happened with Laurel, earlier that year.

As I was leaving the house, I saw Brad sitting on the edge of the bed with his head in his hands. That didn't look good.

When I got there, I could see that her eyes were glazed. Was it the result of drugs or alcohol or both? Her pre-teen daughters were sleeping in a room next to the kitchen where I sat down. She poured me a cup of coffee after offering me a drink telling me I would need one. I couldn't stomach a drink at that time and said that coffee would be okay.

She did not waste time and got right down to the words I never wanted to hear but needed to if I were to face the truth. She was having an affair with my husband and had been for some time.

As I listened numbly, in obvious shock, my mind wandered back to the time in the previous fall, that I had a vision while washing clothes in the basement. I had jumped up to go and find his truck in her yard as I had seen in the vision. That day, I knocked on her door, to be invited in. I saw Brad ducking his head behind a divider. It all was well explained and was logical. He had gone there to see her brother, who was out for a visit. Nothing wrong with that, was there? But then I also went back to the time when I couldn't sleep because he wasn't home but so I went walking down River Road. I caught him riding the bike at midnight coming home from the road where she lived.

She went on to tell me the places they had gone to, and the sinking feeling in my stomach turned to nausea. We had always gone everywhere together, and these were our secret places. They were special and revered, "our" places, and now he had taken her there. Lately, Brad and I hadn't gone anywhere together, and he was taking her to these places now? I had once again been replaced by another woman. Were there more?

> ***You have no idea, lady. There are always "more."***
> ***There "are" many more and always will be***
> ***more! A cheater is a cheater is a cheater!***

When I could speak, I asked her why she was telling me this. In her inebriated state, she blurted out that he was rumoured to have been sleeping with our foster daughter. She was jealous of her and angry with him, and that was why she had told me!

This was so bizarre. Our foster daughter? The teenager with whom we'd been entrusted to be good parents? He was sleeping with her too? But I already knew that, didn't I? I just couldn't face it and still didn't want to believe it. They say betrayal is worse than slow death. At least death makes no promises. We get what we get, but betrayal shatters the heart and destroys the soul. I'd been betrayed by him and my foster daughter. Things couldn't have gotten any worse for me at that moment. I just wanted to die. My mind went back to the night at the farmhouse, which I'd never gotten over. Now I knew my suspicions were true, as there were also other times when he was alone with her, even taking her to Fort Frances to see his grandmother. They had spent two nights in a hotel, and not likely in separate rooms! I wasn't asked to go along but she was asked, and she didn't say no!

With this new information, I knew exactly what had happened, and this woman called me because she was jealous. He was cheating on her, she thought. How bizarre! She was cheating on me with him. What in the world did she expect? Now I knew why he came riding the bicycle at night; he was coming from Danielle's place and unlike his truck, he could hide the bike in some bushes. He was banging her, the woman who was rumoured to be quite promiscuous.

This was too much for me to handle.

As time went on, I learned much due to self-analysis. I wanted to learn so that I'd know how to heal and deal with what I'd gone through. While doing this, I wrote down some of my revelations. I started journaling and writing poetry about feelings, anything to help me heal and get better. Some writings were my theories on things we all talk about but no one really knows for certain, like if there's a God and a devil walking among us on this earth. Or do we just make these things up to explain what we don't totally understand? I was feeling the "evil "when these things started to happen, and I wondered where God was in all of it. But I was always getting the signs; I was just too blind to see and too naive to understand.

For me, it was the unknown, never knowing what to expect from him, never knowing who this man really was, that was driving me around the bend and torturing my mind. I continued to live on an emotional roller coaster. Sometimes I saw a gentle person who cared about others, and at other times I saw a cold, cruel person who just wanted to strike out and hurt someone, and the closest person he felt comfortable hurting was me, his wife, in the sanctity and privacy of our home. Sometimes I thought he was evil when he seemed not to care at all and could do such horrible, torturous things to me with no conscience whatsoever. When his father was around for the first ten years of our marriage, he was likely the victim of Brad's abuse, and I was in a constant honeymoon stage, but when his father left, I took his place as victim, and his "flavour of the day" became the honeymoon in place of me. He treated her like a queen and me like dirt!

At that time, I didn't understand any of it. I just knew it was happening. I knew nothing of the cycle of abuse. In the future, I would start to see the patterns, the cycles and they were all the same but with different results in different situations. Knowing these patterns would have made life easier for me, but these things aren't taught in school or taught to us by our parents. We only find out when we start looking because we know something is drastically wrong or abnormal, but we don't know what it is. What we do realize is that we need to find the answers.

This wasn't the only thing that was happening. It was far more than just abuse! It was far more sinister than anything I could imagine; it was the stuff of nightmares or dreams, like the ones I'd been having. It was worse than the cheating, or lying, or screwing of our foster daughter. It was the evil scheming of the sick, twisted, and crooked mind of a very greedy man, a man who refused to work and had plenty time to scheme and plot. And things would get worse … far, far worse!

It's not going to get any better; it will only get worse. This is the pattern that will be played out. Get out of this relationship while you can, while you're still alive and able to do it!

I didn't listen to this voice in my head, as I was imprisoned by my marriage vows. I was a victim and thought like a victim. As time went on, the verbal blows and the mind games became more frequent and severe. This is how abuse escalates. But for him, in his warped mind, they were all the same, and as soon as the blow was over, it was as though nothing had happened for him. For me, things were building up inside, each adding onto the one before, which I couldn't just forget or treat as though it hadn't happened. It was easier in the honeymoon stage,[13] but when the eggshell walk started and I'd get nervous in anticipation of the next blow, the last ones came back to my mind. I was never to be at ease, never comfortable but always anxious, and there was no such a thing as a peaceful environment in our home anymore like there had been for the first ten years of our marriage. Friends stopped coming to visit, as though they felt the tension in our home. I began to hate my home and felt trapped in it. But at the same time, I couldn't run away, as someone had to take care of it. If I did leave, where would I go? Living with my parents was not an option, as I knew I could not live in the same house as my mother.

Why do you stay in this relationship! Get out while the getting out is good!

I stayed in the relationship because I didn't know anything about abuse! I also didn't know where to go. This was normal for me now, as it was all I knew. I was afraid of being alone! I was to blame for the abuse that's how my brain was programmed to think.

There I was
Stark naked,
Peoples staring
at me, and then
I was alone,
So alone!

I didn't want to be alone. I wanted our nights together, like we'd had in the past. I wanted our love to come back. I valued our wedding vows and wanted to live with him, forever, until "death us do part!" Yikes, I didn't like

---

13   See Appendix for the three stages of the abuse cycle.

the sound of that! Not anymore! Maybe it was the "honeymoons" that kept me there; they were like the sun and the calm coming out after the storm! After all the crap of being in hell, the honeymoons were like heaven, they were so sweet. Was that what I lived for? The honeymoons? A taste of heaven when I could get it? It made me wonder if I was causing the fights just to be able to make up and experience the heaven again.

Until heaven stopped coming!

Now to get back to good, bad and evil, and the spectrum. I could visualize a line drawn with "good" at the left end, "evil" at the right end and "bad" in the middle. At one time in his past, Brad must have been a good person, as I could see this in him from time to time. When he started the manipulation, the cheating, the lying, and the deceitfulness, he did something that took him to the middle--the bad part. If his abuse of me worked for him, then why quit? But bad people have a conscience and awareness that what they're doing isn't right, and they also feel some remorse. When he battered me with horrible words that hurt, he would be sorry later and promise not to do it again. He was aware that what he did was wrong. He had no reason or right to hurt a person, especially someone he claimed to love.

At this point, a person can go back to being good by making the effort, whether it is anger management or counselling, but there is hope of going back to "good." But when the behaviour isn't curbed and keeps going to the other far right end of the spectrum, there is less of a chance this will happen. Unlike with alcoholics, these people don't seem to hit a bottom; they just keeping going, if not with one partner, they'll find another. This was my theory; this was my thinking after hours of analyzing my life.

As a victim, I needed to get out of the situation, but being a victim, I couldn't do it. I saw no recourse and had no backup or support from anyone. I was the silent one. I couldn't tell my best friends about it for two reasons. One, they wouldn't believe me, as Brad could be so nice to others. Two, they felt powerless and wouldn't want to interfere or didn't know what to do. Society allows this abuse to happen and turns a blind eye to it.

At the evil extreme, there is no conscience or remorse. To feel this or go back to being good, their minds need to be reprogrammed and retooled by professionals. Nowadays hypnosis is said to work, and Psychedelics are being experimented with. The evil ones become like serial killers, blow after blow after blow. They get their highs out of hurting people and have to do it. They become more and more narcissistic in nature and will be bolder to see if they can get away with this. Once they do, this will be repeated over and over, as long as they're effective. They won't hurt anyone in front of others, nor will they leave any marks. They're too wary and cunning to do this, as they don't want others to know, nor do they want to get caught. That the name of the game: **do things they enjoy doing and get away with it.** They will set up their spouses to look like they're crazy with their "make crazy" strategies. They just want to hurt, manipulate, and control. They don't care if they hurt someone they love. They may even get off on this or feel a high from inflicting pain on others.

At times when I should have been terrified, I went totally numb, looked him in the eye, and didn't flinch. It was then that he'd back down, and I know that had I flinched, he would have hurt me even more. He needed to know that he was having an effect on me, as that is their way maintaining control of their victims. Often this leads to "overkill" in verbal battering as well. They will be in a rage for a week over something so petty, it's almost a joke, and they always say they're going to "make you pay." For what? And how?

They also use emotional blackmail, which is the transfer of everything you say to them coming back to you in a twisted version, with gross exaggerations or fabrications. You become the eternal scapegoat for everything that goes wrong. You're the reason he wants to kill you; you're the one to blame. After a while, you start believing that you're worthless, and it would be better if you were gotten rid of, making him happy! He has not only dehumanized you, but he now wants to get rid of you. He has tortured your heart and is trying to kill off your soul, your very being, your reason for existing on this earth.

This reminded me of the play of Macbeth and how he reached the ultimate of evil and could even kill children and women. The master of human characteristics, Shakespeare, understood this evil in men and women all too well.

At the evil end, there is no going back.

These men will find a new partner and do exactly the same things to them, or they'll spend the rest of their lives lonely, always scheming how they can do something to someone they have already victimized. Like an addicted person, they're always looking for that first high and thrill they get out of the battering, whether it be physical or verbal. They become addicted to abusing others and conning them, and these abusers never let go. I know of an abuser who kept a voodoo doll, trying to put a hex on his ex-wife to make her suffer after she left him. They never want to see their victims happy, as that angers them. They'd like nothing better than to see us go down and be able to say, "See, I told you!"

We all do things that are considered bad in some point in our lives. There are degrees of bad, but we try to keep that balance. If there were no evil, we wouldn't know any good. It's the spectrum of life, the yin and the yang.

PART 3:
'Til Death Us Do Part

Chapter 21: The Discovery

God does work in strange ways. I could not conceive, no matter how hard I tried.

My mind would often go back to the little three-year-old boy who came into my life and heart. Why did God take him away from me? My husband had become interested in children, little babies, and young people. Why didn't he fight to keep Ricky? Why did he interfere by talking to the social worker in secret? What did he really say to her to make her take Ricky away?

I remembered when we were ready to adopt a little three-year-old girl as well. Our lives were becoming complete, and all had been falling into place. I was incredibly happy in our tenth year of marriage, as I thought this was the family I was going to have. I was so wrong! Both foster children were taken away by my husband's actions, some of them unknown to me at the time.

But this was also a blessing. Before Ricky left, Brad was looking after him and taking him to the farm while I was at work. One day when riding in the truck with Brad and our son, Ricky acted strangely. He seemed to fear that we were going to leave him in the truck alone. What was Brad doing to Ricky when I was away at work and he was looking after him? Later on, I heard rumours that Ricky had been left in the truck alone, even when it was cold, while Brad went to see his lady friends. In retrospect, after what happened with Laurel, perhaps it was just as well that Ricky was taken away. Things aren't always what they seem, my father told me. What was this man I'd married and had loved? An evil monster who abused children? Was he sick in the head? Why could I not see this earlier? Why did I not realize he was wearing a mask, and the man behind the mask was just the opposite of what I was seeing?

Now there were soon to be no children in the picture, Ralph was gone. Laurel had moved out and had an apartment of her own. Ricky would never come back, as he had moved with his father and new mother to BC. The adoption applications for Ricky and the little girl were cancelled. This was another sign of what was to come. Or was it just another part of a master scheme to get rid of me, so as not to have to pay support or alimony? I was all that stood in his way, all that was left. No father, no children, just me.

Face it, lady, he doesn't want to have children--not with you--and there's a good reason for that. His eyes are roving, and he's a self-serving person who doesn't really care about a family, or children, or a wife. He only cares about himself and the one thing he really wants. Don't you know what it is? Figure it out and be careful. This man has a plan, a scheme, and you are part of his master plan. Beware! You're doomed if you don't wake up in time and protect yourself!

He had obviously been chasing my foster daughter and was not hiding it anymore. One time I caught him with his hand on her knee. They were always going somewhere together, and I started feeling like a stranger in my own home. She'd sit on the couch, and he'd be on the other one, while I'd sit in a chair, feeling totally left out.

After the incident with Laurel at the farm house, I was a basket case. That was the first event that led to traumatic stress later in life, and the second event was being told about the affair with Danielle. The third shock was still to come.

Death or torture? Which could be worse?

Night without air,
A pillow over my face,
My God, I can't breathe!
There was a strong arm on my neck holding me down on the bed.

I was going to die!
Don't fight,
It's no use,
He is trying to kill me!
Scream!
I can't,
Air, I need air!

Post-traumatic stress is like experiencing something so hurtful and painful, you can never get it out of your mind. You have nightmares, you think about it constantly, you get depressed, you can't sleep or eat, and you act compulsively. It never goes away. It's always there, like the grief of losing someone close to you. You go on with a normal life, but it's always there, ready to erupt like a volcano if it's agitated and sensitive buttons are pushed.

I thought back to my "preview" thing that was so obvious and also scary as a child. Or was it my guardian angel giving me signs, like going to the farm and finding the imprint of the letter and the phone call in the middle of the night? There were now two women involved: a sixteen-year-old, and Danielle. Were there more? He had all day to do things while I was working. He was not coming home at night and making excuses that when he took cattle into the stockyards, he had to stay in Winnipeg overnight, as he was too tired to drive home. Always the excuses!

When I went back to my doctor at the Selkirk Psychiatric Hospital, I told him all that had happened, and he told me that he'd been treating me for the wrong thing; I was being treated for paranoia, but now I was finally seeing the truth, and the truth was killing me day after day. This cheating went on for the next four years. Brad felt pretty proud of himself, while making me feel like the most unattractive, unloved, useless person in the world. I was to blame for his cheating, of course. I should never have let him get started, he told others. Once he did, there was no feeling of guilt, so there was no stopping it. It becomes like an addiction that takes on a life of its own, an obsession that he couldn't stop or was it done to drive me around the bend? He felt no guilt, because in his mind I was at fault for his cheating, and this to him was quite normal.

I didn't know exactly when he'd started, as he'd lied and told me I was imagining things whenever I got even a little suspicious. It could have been going on for years while I was half an hour away, working, and he had to take cattle into Winnipeg, or was at the farm with nothing to do other than a few chores in winter. The doctor gave me the name of a lawyer, but he also said that Brad might be going through his change of life, which can be hard on a wife. Later, I wished he hadn't told me this, as it gave me a false ray of hope to hang on to. I took my marriage vows seriously and was hoping for help for both of us. I didn't want to end a marriage that for ten years had seemed so perfect. This change of life normally lasts five years, the doctor said, and it's hell for women. This gave me reason to doubt and put off what I should have done, which was take action. I went to a lawyer, and he told me to strike while the iron was hot, but instead I gave Brad the benefit of the doubt, another sign of my lack of knowledge about abuse.

I was still hoping that he would be willing to go for help, that he would feel remorse, and that we would live happily ever after when his "midlife crisis" was over. Hopefully he'd realize what he had in me--a good person and a loving wife. Fat chance! This was my second worst mistake. My first was marrying that man in the first place. I stayed on, and it did not get better. Now I know it never would have, as he needed help. He almost went for help on his own once. I so wish he had! Going for help would have proven him in the wrong, and a narcissist's brain is wired so that he can never be wrong. He was always right. He told me this all the time, and one time he cracked a joke about it: **He was only wrong one time in his life, and that was when he thought he was wrong!**

By then, our thirteenth year of marriage, I had found a job for Laurel and she'd left to live in an apartment, as things were too tense in the house. But that didn't stop him, as he was seen taking a bottle in a bag to the apartment where she lived. But at least it wasn't happening in my house. He hardly came home for any length of time anymore.

Chapter 22: The Cheating Game

Then Patricia came into the picture. Most of his women were old flames from the past, and he just couldn't get enough of them! Every night he'd put on his nice leather motorcycle jacket I'd bought him, splash cologne on his face, jingle the keys (making sure I heard them), and take off for somewhere. He did the key jingling on purpose to taunt me. One day, he just smugly said, "I'm going out to look after my love affairs." It made me feel like the ugliest and dumbest woman on earth. He no longer wanted me, and I was nothing to him anymore. The others were more exciting; they were new "old" flames, and it was exciting to rekindle these sparks. Later, I realized that he might have had a low self-worth because women in the past had rejected him, and now he had to prove he still had it and that they really wanted him.

The intrigue was like a high for him. Maybe there was another high as well, one caused by "weed," but at that time I didn't know enough about drugs to recognize the symptoms. I felt so sick to my stomach; I wanted to retch at times. Nothing ever changed; it was the same thing every night when he did come back to our house. He came home, had supper, jingled the keys, and took off. Sometimes he came home the next day, and sometimes not for a few days. Life was hell for me. I didn't know what to do, what this man wanted from me, or why he was treating me this way. I felt totally helpless, out of control, and sick. I wouldn't find out until later why he was doing this to me. It just happened to be part of his Plan B to drive me insane so that I'd have an emotional breakdown. Plan A, was to get rid of me through murder.

I couldn't stand being alone anymore, so one night I rode the bike over to the place where he left the tractor and bailer in the field often enough to make this look suspicious. The plausible excuse I had ready as an explanation was that a man had come to the house to look for him, but the truth was that I really wanted to see what he was doing there. There was a house trailer near this field where a number of unhappy wives retreated every summer. This was heaven for him: three or four hormonally charged women, unhappy with their marriages and wanting an affair. Some even wanted babies at the twenty-third hour of their productive life. He was ready for them all. I wanted to find him, but the place was quite dark. I walked around toward the back, where I could hear voices. I stopped to listen and heard him say, "What do I do to get rid of her? Shoot her? I admit I'm a greedy SOB …"

I didn't wait to hear anymore, as I recognized his voice. The words shook me to the very core of my being. I appeared so they would notice I was there, and then took off. I could hardly ride my bike home, going from left to right on the road like a drunk. I finally reached home, went to bed, and tried to hide under the covers. I was in total shock. He had seen me and came home later to scold me for being a snoop. No apology, no remorse for what he'd said, just the cold shoulder treatment because I'd dared to go to his "harem" and make a fool of myself … and of course, embarrass him in front of these women by showing up. This doesn't do a lot for a woman's self-worth! To suddenly realize the man you've loved for so many years wants to kill you! To shoot you! To get rid of you like a possession he no longer needs! A disposable commodity! This was now the second time, he had indicated by letter, and then words, that he wanted *to get rid of me.*

I knew he had several rifles hidden somewhere at the farmhouse or in the garage. Was my life in danger? I didn't think so. I thought they were just stupid words from a stupid man who was trying to impress some stupid women. I later went to the same trailer and approached one of the women by the name of Cindy. She wasn't the one he was seeing, but I was feeling out of sorts and asked her if her husband cheated on her too. She said, "All the time, but I do too. We cheat on each other." The cheating game, where there are no winners, only losers, like in mind games. Cheating games and love triangles could be the seeds sown for murder.

Chapter 23: It **Never** Stopped!

*T*his went on all summer. One day I was at the farm hauling hay bales when I met him going the other way. He stopped and gave me instructions as to some other bales he wanted me to haul. He was in his convertible, dressed all sporty and looking smug. There was a towel in the back. *Beach!* I thought. But I was not invited. After a few hours of hauling hay, I went home. I could stand it no longer. I'd figured out from some incidents that this woman's name was Patricia, and I also knew her last name and that she lived in the city. I looked up a number in the phone book and called her husband to let him know his wife was with my husband and that I figured they gone to the beach. He lived in Winnipeg, but he told me he was heading out to the trailer. I waited at home, and then the convertible returned with a big dent in the driver's side fender. A woman's wet bathing suit was still in the back seat. He was furious and told me that her husband, who had met them at the gate, had almost killed him. Later I found out that the husband had taken a hammer to the car. This didn't stop the affair; it went on for the rest of the summer. But she wasn't the only one; there was another one, called Tammy, who lived on River Road as well.

When winter came toward the end of our thirteenth year of marriage, I was told to see my parents for Christmas, but he wouldn't be coming. I knew he was going to carry on with Patricia while I was gone, and maybe even bring her to our house. But what could I do? I spent a nice quiet Christmas with my parents, and he spent it with his friends and lover. I had picked up the phone and heard him make his plans. He would be with his friends Roy and Debra, who lived in a neighboring town. They were also close friends with Patricia.

It eventually petered out, and this woman became involved with another man, but the cheating never stopped. It went from one woman to the next. I got reports almost every day about him being seen with some woman in his truck. The farm was being neglected, calves were dying in the cold, and nothing was getting done around home. Womanizing was now his new career or pastime. Still, I hoped that it would soon be over, this change of life. I stuck by him like a good woman should and put up with it, but the pain inside of me was becoming unbearable. A human being can only put up with so much pain before they start doing crazy things. I felt totally powerless. I couldn't leave him, as I couldn't leave my home. He had to be the one to leave! But why should he? He had the best of both worlds: a wife and he could also be a philanderer and get away with it. I was nothing! I had nothing to live for anymore, so I just existed, but with my heart tearing into tiny shreds day by day.

I joined Al Anon. I didn't know if he was an alcoholic, but my pain was the same, and I needed some support. This helped me get through the worst of it, which was still to come. Some things happened that I could never reveal to anyone except the law enforcement officers, and they wouldn't listen.

Chapter 24: Suspicious Happenings

During this very difficult time, other strange things had been happening. My mind kept going back to things that I felt were suspicious in attempting to figure them out. My nephew, from Beardmore, Ontario was coming to spend the summer with us in 1982, because his parents, my brother and his wife, were having marital problems. Our problems were still covered up, and we functioned like a normal couple in the eyes of those who knew us and also those who did not really know us. Brad would put on a good front when we had guests in the house. Jimmy was seventeen, tall and lanky with platinum-blond hair and green eyes like his mother. He helped us on the farm and enjoyed staying at our place, where he could fish and swim whenever he felt like it. We had a nice place for young people to have fun. He didn't miss his friends, as he seemed a bit of a recluse. His mother was eccentric. She was into astrology, ghosts, and the paranormal, and I thought she might be schizophrenic. So when her son started having delusions at my home, I thought he had inherited this trait from his mother. I was wrong once again.

There was no reason to suspect Jimmy was taking drugs, or that Brad had supplied them, but Brad was the only person Jimmy knew in town that might have access to drugs. Jimmy also had saved up some money so he could afford to pay for them. Was Brad secretly a drug peddler, as money was so important to him? I came home one day from blueberry picking and found Jimmy in the basement, burning incense. I thought this was odd but was likely because he'd been smoking, so I gave him heck for that. His parents told me, they did not allow him to smoke. Jimmy and I, later, had a discussion about drugs, and he tried to convince me that it was all right to take them. I gave him a lecture on drugs, dramatizing the effects of them, from what I had heard, so he'd be scared and not think they were cool. He seemed to be listening intently to me, and I saw a strange look on his face. Oh my God, I thought later, was he on drugs already? Was that what he was trying to cover up with incense? I had a bad feeling in my gut, and my gut was right 99 per cent of the time.

Something was going on with Jimmy, but of course no one knew what, or no one would tell me, if they did know. He went back home to Beardmore, Ontario and said he'd be coming back the next summer when he was through with school. Next spring, I picked up a letter from him addressed to Brad and wondered why it wasn't addressed to me, as I was his aunt. I opened the letter. It read that Jimmy was looking forward to coming to see Brad, not me. I thought that odd. What did Brad have that was so appealing to Jimmy? It seemed weird. Something wasn't right. Another sign?

Something isn't right, so why can't you read the signs yet?

Then my brother called me late one night. He was beside himself with worry. Jimmy had not come home that night. The next few days were traumatic, as a three-hundred-person search party and dogs were out looking for Jimmy for the entire weekend. Another call from my brother came three days later. He had found Jimmy unconscious, lying on the ground. He was easy to spot, as he always wore bright blue shirts. He revived James and then literally carried a 6' 2", 180-pound youth over his shoulder and out of the bush, stopping to revive him several times along the way.

My brother later told me that he thought Jimmy had gone into withdrawal, that he had been on drugs and tried to quit on his own, and the DTs were the effect of it. Jimmy went to hide in the bush and then got bush whacky, thus hiding from his rescuers. They had found a cabin with blood all over the floor and then tracks leading into a stream, but none coming out. He was making a conscious effort not to be found. He had stab marks all over his head when he was found, as though he'd attempted to kill himself. In Ontario, when a person appears to be suicidal, or on drugs, they'll be placed in a psychiatric institution for observation. Jimmy was rushed to facility in Thunder Bay. He'd been there for almost a month when Brad piped up one day and said that he was going to see him. I found it strange that he would want to see Jimmy when he wouldn't even go in to see his father when he was hospitalized.

The night before he left, I heard him talk in his sleep, and he said he felt guilty about what was happening to Jimmy! I thought that was strange and wondered what had triggered it. When Brad came back, he told me that they were going to keep him there until they had adjusted his medications. It was getting close to the end of the school year, which was my busiest and most stressful time as a teacher. On the last day of school, late at night, I got another call from my brother.

Jimmy was dead.

Apparently, he had been on the highway headed to Manitoba and had been hit by a car on the main highway. The police and news reports showed a picture of the police car and a hat lying on the far side of the expressway. According to reports, his hat had blown off his head and he was running to retrieve it, right into the path of an oncoming car.

But why was he out on the highway in the first place? He had gone to get a haircut, and on that particular morning the staff at the ward, had let him have his clothes and shoes. He went to the barber, waited for a while, and then took off. Two hours later, Jimmy became a statistic. He was well along the highway and seemed to be hitchhiking to Manitoba to come and see us. Why wasn't he going home first, north instead of west? It wasn't until later years that I wondered if he was being supplied with "weed" for a price when he'd visited the previous summer, and if Brad's visit to him was to get him to keep that quiet by promising him more weed when he got to our house. If that were the case, I could understand Brad's feeling of guilt and the letter addressed to him and not me. Addictions are stronger than anything in a person's life, stronger than family, a career, and love.

Only the Creator knows all the answers. Was Jimmy's trek to the bush caused by withdrawal or the powerful effects of drugs? Was he suicidal when he ran in front of the car? I did not think so, as he was on his way to Manitoba. However he may have been on drugs to deal with his withdrawal. When first questioned after he recovered from his time in the bush, he didn't know what had happened to him. He was in a state of confusion, or perhaps he didn't want to know or tell. This will remain one of life's secrets. When one doesn't see any way of finding the answers, one has to put the questions into the recesses of their mind so that they can handle all the other things coming down on them. These things, however, are never forgotten.

When I went to find Brad at the farmhouse after my brother's phone call, a man came running out of the bush. The man seemed to know Brad. He was out of breath and told me he was an informant for the RCMP and he showed me his NARC card. He also showed me a slash scar on his side, where he'd been knifed. He seemed totally out of it, so I didn't know whether to believe him or not. But why did he have a card with NARC and a phone number on it? Brad had some things to do at the farm, so I took this confused man to our log house on River Road and poured coffee for him to sober him up. It was the first time I witnessed DTs, as he was shaking all over. I had never seen them before, but I suspected that's what they were.

He seemed to be going into a seizure and said he needed alcohol. I found some wine in the fridge and gave him some to drink. He got better. Later, Brad came to take him home. I started to wonder where the man had come from, who had dropped him off, and why was he going to the farmhouse. Was this unoccupied house at the farm the supply house for dope, and was Brad the supplier? Was he too cunning to do the deal in front of me? Did I know so little about illegal drugs and the drug trade? The strange man seemed in dire need of dope. I never did get to learn his name, and I never saw this man again. Shortly after that, I was barred from the farm, forbidden to go there. A cable was put across the entrance to the farmhouse, and I was told I wasn't allowed in. Why? Things were becoming weirder and weirder. It was the stuff fiction is made of, not real life. Or could life be a novel?

Everything seemed so surreal!

A few months later, a couple of young men came to visit me and said they had something to tell me. They told me there were things going on at farmhouse and that I was better off not knowing about it, but I should just stay away from it. Edward, a neighbor, also told me a few things about the house, and he seemed too scared to tell me much more than he did. While talking to me, he kept looking around, and kept his voice very low. What was really going on? I was starting to be afraid to go there, and even afraid of staying in the log house on River Road.

Chapter 25: Arson

I would still go to the farm the odd time, in spite of the cable, and just go through a back gate to get to the house, but not as often as I used to. The house was locked up tight. I was never allowed to have a key! Then more strange things started happening. Cars were being brought to the farm in the middle of the night. Many cars. It was the fifteenth summer of our relationship. I'd go and look into these cars. They were full of tools and other items.

When chasing Patricia and other women at the infamous trailer on Baker Drive, Brad was friends with Roy and Debra. Debra was the owner of this trailer. Roy had an auto body shop in Selkirk, so I wondered if the cars were coming from his place. Were they the storage bunkers for other expensive things, like tools? Soon I heard that his shop had burned to the ground, and Roy had lost everything, according to the newspaper. He applied for insurance, but then one night Brad was talking in his sleep about helping Roy set the fire. I was shocked, but Roy got away with it and received a nice insurance cheque for all the cars and equipment he'd had claimed he had lost in the fire. Was a fire the reason all the stuff that had been brought to the farm, was to hide them, and then later moved to a different location? I told the police about all the cars. They came to look at them but did nothing. Then all the cars disappeared.

I started to suspect my husband was an informant to the RCMP, as they didn't arrest him for any of the criminal things that I suspected he was doing. I knew he was a thief, as I was in the car when he went through old buildings to look for antiques earlier in our marriage. He indoctrinated me into thinking he was right to do this because he was poor and could take from the rich;

he could make excuses for anything. We had become a Bonnie and Clyde; I was his assistant. When he left me to move in with Cindy, I took back all the items that were around the house that he had stolen. I went back to being my old self, and honesty was a virtue I learned from my father. I had kept my mouth shut for years but now, when so much was happening, it was starting to hit me. **He was a thief.** Could he also be a murderer and have attempted to murder his father? Was he planning to murder me as well? Could he be involved with drug dealers or be one himself? The connection with the man who came out of the bush was too coincidental, and then one day I overheard Brad reporting marijuana plants in a friend's house to an RCMP officer he was buddies with. Was he this officer's informant, and was this why he could get away with so much and never be investigated or charged? I wondered about this, but never found out and likely never will. What kind of man had I married? Seriously? What went on in that evil mind of his?

Then I was told that he was using Laurel as a prostitute at the farmhouse after getting her drunk. The neighbour, Edward, let this slip too; but I couldn't believe it was true until later when I saw the true colours of the man I was married to. Even though there was no proof of it, he was quite capable of doing such horrific things. He would do anything for an easy buck. I liked to analyze people to see why they would do the things they do and then come up with theories. I also got to think about my instincts, as well as from the hidden crevices of my subconscious and intuitive mind. I came up with another theory:

> ***It's not true that we get to know the person when we live with them. We don't get to really know them until we split up with them and the mask comes off as they no longer need to use a mask!***

When abusers no longer need us to be their prey, they find someone else, usually someone with more money. That wouldn't have been hard for Brad, as I had put every cent into paying off the farm loans and buying cattle, more land and machinery. By the time we were finally free of debt, I was penniless, and the new woman would have money as well as a nice settlement from her husband and perhaps even support if she didn't work. All the women he sought out were divorcees.

Chapter 26: What Really Happened to Ralph?

I started to wonder what had really happened to Ralph, so I called Brad's stepbrother about it. He lived in Winnipeg. They never did get along and didn't keep in touch, but I found Larry's number and called him. It turned out that he was the one who'd demanded that Ralph be taken to Winnipeg, because he feared for Ralph's life after the blow to his head. Apparently, the doctor told Larry that he had called Brad, when Ralph was in the Pinawa hospital and Brad had said to him, "If I go near that bastard, I'll kill him!" I also told him that there was a statute of limitations on assault, as I had already checked that out with the local RCMP. Larry remarked that it hadn't been an assault but attempted murder, and there is no statute of limitations on that! Was that why Brad would not go to the hospital with me to see Ralph? Did he fear that Ralph would recognize who hit him on the head?

I was shocked, so I went to the hospital to check the medical records. The doctors had determined that Ralph had been hit on the head with a blunt two-by-four. I was advised by the doctor not to pursue anything, as there was no point by that time; there would not be enough evidence to prove anything. Nothing was ever done about it, but I knew exactly who had the motive, who was starting to show greed, and who would want to inherit everything as soon as possible. After all, there were two stepsiblings and a partner involved. Shortly after being hurt, Ralph had wanted to go to BC to live. I think he was afraid that whoever had hit him would come back to finish the job. Maybe he even had a suspect but was too afraid to name him. Going to BC was a drastic move for a person his age; especially when most of his family was here and he only had a sister living there.

Brad's motive, of course, was to get the land before the step siblings had a chance at it, and Brad did get it signed over to him when Ralph went to BC, so this plan worked. If there was foul play involved and Brad was the perpetrator as I suspected, then he got away with a major crime. But I still didn't want to believe this of the man I loved. It was too bizarre. I couldn't get my head around someone being manipulative to the point of being downright evil.

He is trying to con you, lady. Wake up and smell the coffee. Are you really that naive?

I was that naive! My mind didn't want to believe it. Our minds aren't to be trusted; our gut is more reliable. My gut was doing a lot of twists and turns and feeling nauseated, and I was would be sick every time I would see Brad, whom I was getting to see less and less.

Chapter 27: The Subject for Nightmares

Night without air
A pillow over my face
My God, I can't breathe
I AM going to die,
Any minute now!
I am going to die!

Why was I having these dreams of a pillow over my face? Was he going to kill me? No, that couldn't be possible. This wasn't the city, and he wasn't that insane or cruel. He wasn't a killer! Or could he be? One never knows what goes on in other people's heads unless they can somehow get into them. Some people just don't think like the rest of us. To some, killing another person is normal, and they wonder why the rest of us don't want to do the same. To them, we aren't normal. They are the normal ones! I couldn't profile him, and I guess I really didn't want to, being afraid of what I'd find. We don't want to face the truth, if we don't want our illusions destroyed, especially if the truth is of an evil nature.

So he was getting his father to sign over the farm to him. Was this not motive for murder? To get his inheritance? No, not Brad! He wouldn't do that sort of thing, not that gentle, soft-spoken man. Or would he? My mind took on a great deal of doubt, but I was usually a head-together person and didn't wish to become paranoid and live in fear. I should have listened to my doubts and, most of all, my gut. I became imprisoned in my mind because of resorting to denial.

> *He has always been abusive to his father. Can't you see that? Are you that blind or naïve? He has plenty of motive to kill. Can't you see how greedy he is?*

No, I can't! This, of course, was more like, "I don't want to!"

This went on for a total of four years (that I knew of), the cheating, lying, the paranoia, and for me, the fear. My health was deteriorating. Along with the mystery disease, my mind felt sick, my stomach felt sick, and then another strange thing happened. He didn't come to my parents' home with me to see them at Christmas for a number of years. But as soon I told him about moving my parents out of their house and into a nursing home in December of 1983, he was on the radar again, living back at home and showing interest in spending Christmas with my family in Swan River, even if it was in the nursing home.

I'd gone alone earlier in December to move my parents and then again at Christmas, meeting up with my brother and his family. Brad came with me at Christmas, which was odd to me. My father did some strange things that Christmas. He'd always been so independent while looking after my mother after she had a stroke. He never wanted to move into a seniors' home or a nursing home. However, before Christmas he asked me to move them into this home, after both of them had been hospitalized for a while. I moved them in early December, leaving their house empty.

I had a feeling my father knew something I didn't know and was doing this for Mother, as she wasn't capable of looking after herself. He had also asked me about Brad at that time, when I moved my parents into the home. My father always knew when things were plaguing me and made the point of asking if I was silent. When I first told my father about Brad's cheating, I heard him utter profanities for the very first time in my life. I had always been Daddy's little girl! And I still was his girl! I was happy to be able to tell him things were better, and that Brad had come home to sleep with me again. My father was happy. I was glad to leave him with this happiness and not have to tell him what happened a few months later, after my father passed away.

My brother and his wife arrived to spend Christmas with us as well, using the house while Mother and my father were in the seniors' home. When I got back to my home on January 9, 1984, I received a call to let me know that my father had passed away. So we all packed up again and went back to Swan River to arrange his funeral. Mother refused to go that day, and that was all right. We had the funeral service in the Anglican Church. What really shocked me was that Brad came with me. Again I wondered why? I also found it strange that he was being so nice to me. Things went well for a while, but Brad seemed disappointed that the will my father had made left everything to my mother, even though I had been named the Power of Attorney and the executor. We got nothing then, as my mother was still living and would be for another three years. I guess he hadn't expected this.

Things started falling apart again, and Brad often didn't come home at night. I had taken the school year off, as I was very tired and stressed out. I also thought that staying home, would give me a chance to see what was really going on, at home. In spring, I got very sick with a bad cold that turned into pneumonia. I also suffered mentally, and became a basket case once again, needing to be hospitalized a number of times. When I had pneumonia, another strange thing started happening to me. I felt like I wasn't able to breathe at times. I'd start vomiting and think I was having a heart attack. I'd try so hard to breathe to get oxygen into my lungs. I even went outside to walk around the yard, taking gulps of fresh air. I found out from a doctor that this was hyperventilation, which became a common thing with me and usually happened when I'd see Brad again. I learned from the doctor that I needed to breathe into a paper bag instead of gulping for air. That's how I managed my hyperventilating. While I was lying in bed, feeling sick and unable to eat because of my pneumonia, Brad walked in during the middle of the day. I hadn't eaten for several days and couldn't get up to make myself anything to eat. He had not come for days and seemed to have little concern for me.

He saw me in bed and proceeded to take off his clothes, crawling into bed with me. I wondered what was wrong with him, as we hadn't had sex in a long, long time, What could possibly turn a man on when seeing his wife as sick as I was? I didn't want sex but complied because I was too weak to fight him off. That was when I discovered something else about him. He wanted perverse sex, even doing the anal thing. I was too sick to argue or say no, and just felt the pain of his new thing. I realized then that I had actually been sexually assaulted by my own husband. Who would believe a wife filing a complaint that her husband had sexually assaulted her? Of course, I don't think I could have said no; I had no voice. The police would not arrest anyone for sexual assault if the victim had not said, no!

Everything always seemed to be in his favor, he could do what he wanted to me, hurt me physically, sexually, emotionally, and financially and no one cared, as there were no witnesses or marks on my body to prove anything. When he'd hit me, he'd use a soft phone book, which left no marks. He was very careful. The next day, after this assault, my neighbour walked in and brought me a bowl of soup. That was the day I started to recover, after eating the nourishing soup. Again, I felt that he bad wanted me to die or hoped I would.

Chapter 28: Was This for Real?

Later, that same spring after my father passed away, I was lying in bed and hurting emotionally one night after he'd been gone for a few days. Where had he been? My heart was aching so much I started talking and couldn't stop when he came into the bedroom. I was once again reacting to the emotional pain inflicted with his constant cheating on me and the neglect I was feeling. Suddenly, he placed a pillow over my head as I was lying on my left side in bed. He put his arm across my neck to hold me down. What was going on? A pillow over my mouth so I was having difficulty breathing! An arm was crunching into my neck, so I couldn't move away or move the pillow from my face! It suddenly hit me; he was trying to smother me. **He was trying to kill me!** I was in shock. I went numb and quit struggling, but it was no use. I was feeling closed in and thought to myself. *This is it! I'm going to die, I will die. This is how murder victims must feel before they die! This is the real thing; this is no joke. This is very, very real.*

He is trying to kill you. Face it; he's trying to kill you! This could end up being your murder!

I was numb and couldn't believe it was really happening. It was so bizarre, like I was a character in a movie or a novel. I was someone else, not me! But my breath was getting shallower, and it felt like I was passing out. *A nice way to go* was my last thought, as there was no pain except in my neck. Then he suddenly got up, pulled the pillow off my face and I was able to move. "I am not going to jail for your murder!" he said. He actually said the word, *murder*. But of course, there was no one to hear, no witnesses. So he was trying to murder me! It was over, and I tried to sleep with him beside me, but sleep wouldn't come. I was still numb, like I was living in a dream, or perhaps a nightmare would be a better word. Yet, I was so calm, so "deadly" calm. I was a Super Zombie living in Fantasyland, a land of surreal. This was all a figment of my imagination, I thought! It had to be!

That was the first attempt on my life, but not the last. It was attempted murder, but I didn't think of it as such at the time, not until later in my life. I should have gone to the police, but they'd never believed me before, so why would they believe me now? Of course, there would be no witnesses. There never are! There were no marks, as a pillow doesn't leave any marks. It was only my word against his, and he was their buddy, so they wouldn't touch him, I thought. I was just a nut case, a disgruntled wife, seeing a shrink and looking for something to hold against my husband with whom I was no longer happy. What could I say, that would make any difference? Who would believe me? This was just too bizarre!

No one cares, Lady. There is no one who will care that you can tell! No one will believe you!

This was the beginning of the "silence". There was no one I could tell, no one who would really care, except my friends, and I couldn't tell them. I didn't wish to alarm them, and they couldn't possibly understand what I was going through. They were all happily married, or happily single! No one wanted to take their life away from them. So what was my life really worth? It made me feel so worthless after years of thinking I'd done well, worked hard, and gotten somewhere in life. Was this to be my reward for loving, trusting, and caring? Death? Superwoman was going to die soon! And when she does, Brad would have everything we owned, in his name. Plan A!

Plan A didn't work, so it was now time for Plan B. Look out, lady, this isn't over yet!

This caused me to do strange things in the next while. Sometimes I was afraid to be home alone. If he was in one of his moods, or I was about to react badly to the way he was treating me, I didn't feel safe. I would go to visit a friend and ask if I could stay there for a night or two. No questions were ever asked, a bed was made for me, and I was welcome and felt safe. One time my hosts and I discovered footprints, large ones, in the flower bed outside of their window. I knew Brad had extra-large feet! These footprints were very noticeable in the soft mud just outside the screen door. We realized someone knew where I was! Someone was outside at night, spying on me and listening to our conversation through the open windows or the screen door. This was even scarier, and now it involved people I loved. I no longer felt safe there either. I discovered Osborne House, a woman's shelter in Winnipeg, where I spent a couple of nights when I was too afraid to go home.

A possible earlier attempt. Sometimes the mind blocks things and it takes something else to trigger off memories and make sense of them.

I started to remember, a year earlier, another incident that could have been an attempt to murder me. It happened in the middle of winter, a very cold forty-below night. The wood stove was nice and cozy when the heat came up from the basement. It was burning well. At eight o'clock, I was ready for bed, while Brad was already sleeping in the living room in front of the TV. Shortly after falling asleep, I was awakened by a crackling sound in the closet of our bedroom. I smelled heat! I opened the closet door. The chimney pipes from the wood stove went through the closet. They were fiery red and crackling with the heat. There were flames in the ceiling above the chimney. In alarm, I called the fire department, and trucks were sent out. As a child, I had a phobia of fires, a phobia that never left me. I was so frightened. The firefighters came and put out the fire. On their way out, their words hit me: "Keep an eye on it; the fire might start up again!"

The men had cut a hole in the wall outside on the gable end of the house to put the fire out above the ceiling and under the roof. Brad said he was going to get some insulation to fill the hole as it would get cold at night, especially around forty below. As he drove out of the driveway with the only vehicle plugged in that night, the words of the firemen were like a knife thrust into my heart. The fire may start up again! I was alone! I was all alone in the middle of an extremely cold night.

He was leaving me alone in a house that could burn down, with no vehicle that would start. We were eight kilometers from town. I started to panic as I waited for him to come back. I kept running into the closet to look for red flames. I started to clean the mess left by the firemen, to keep my mind from thinking about fires. Two hours later, after midnight, and he still wasn't home! My panic grew into extreme angst. Maybe it was going to be like the other nights; maybe he was going to spend a night with some woman! My mind started racing, my heart was pounding, and I couldn't take it any longer. I had to get out. I tried to start my car, but it wouldn't start. The car had not been plugged in. I went back into the house and was met by the smell of smoke and the dirty, wet bedroom carpet. Panic took over, so I put on my coat and started the eight kilometre walk to town to stay in a hotel room rather than in the house … alone! It was frigid out and hauntingly still. Everything was deadly quiet, no cars, and no wind. Only the moon, so it was easy to see where I was going.

Just as I got over the Winnipeg River Bridge, a truck was coming toward me. It was the first vehicle I'd seen, after walking half a kilometre. It was Brad. He stopped when he saw me. At first, I was happy to see him and that he was coming home two hours later but he was coming home! I jumped into the truck and then the verbal battering started. I was an f'ing idiot, walking to town. What the hell was wrong with me? I had the brains of a two-year old! I was f'ing crazy!

I put up my hand automatically to deflect the verbal blows, but being in trauma already, I couldn't handle it. I jumped out of the truck and started to run to get over the fence I thought I saw. I was escaping! Suddenly, I realized we were on the bridge, and I was going over the railing, not a fence! I felt myself falling and grabbed onto the bridge with both hands, hanging over the side. I looked up and saw Brad looking down at me, but he did nothing to grab my hands! They say you see your life go by before you die. This was not true for me. In that moment, all I could think was why isn't he grabbing my hands? Does he want me to fall and die? Of course, I already knew the answer, but at that moment I thought he would rescue me. He didn't even look worried or alarmed. My hands were starting to freeze as I had no mitts on, and suddenly my grip let go, and down I went. I felt excruciating pain and the wind knocked out of me. I heard a loud cracking sound and wondered if I'd cracked the ice, as the river seldom froze over, under the Winnipeg River Bridge. I was very cold, but the ice would still be thin under the bridge. I couldn't get up at first. I just wanted to get home and get to bed, but walking was almost impossible, so I had to crawl.

When I managed to stand up, I couldn't put weight on my left leg. I dragged myself up the sides of the river bank into the truck, and when I got home, I dragged myself down the stairs to sleep in the basement, as I couldn't sleep in the bedroom on the main floor after the fire and the damage done to the carpets. The next day, I knew I needed to go to the hospital. They x-rayed my hip and said there was a hairline crack in it and I was told I had to stay in the hospital for two weeks.

They put me on a machine to lift me into the bathtub, which was highly embarrassing for me, being the independent person I always was. Super Woman should not need to be lifted into a bathtub! Then they fitted me with crutches. I was in terrible pain but asked for a typewriter, as it was the end of semester and I had to type out and deliver the exams to my students.

Three days later, I signed myself out of the hospital against my doctor's advice and went back to work so I could deliver my exams. Brad came to pick me up. As we drove over the bridge, I was shocked! Below the bridge where I had fallen was open water! How lucky I was to be alive! How lucky I was that it was frozen over enough that night to hold me, even though I had fallen from at least forty feet or more! Was that loud crack I'd heard; the ice cracking or my hip fracturing? But I survived, and I realized that I must have a guardian angel looking after me who saved my life! I was happy to be alive, although times were not happy for me at all. The feeling of being grateful only lasted a few days.

A couple of weeks later, two friends of Brad's came to the house. They walked into the house, but Brad wasn't home. I felt that they were expecting things from me. After all, when a man cheats on his wife, she's fair game for all men who are looking for a one-night stand! She must be needy, and if he's cheating on her, she would likely be happy to do the same to him! What a crock! But this was the mentality of some men in my town, I thought. And who knew what Brad had been telling people? Maybe he told them that I was good in bed, or that it was all right for them to come and see me, or maybe he even paid them off to do it so he could come home and catch me cheating. He wasn't above setting me up for things like that. They sat at the table, drinking and waiting. For what? I could only guess. They had brought in their own liquor so I felt uncomfortable with them getting more and more inebriated. Then one of them, told me the story Brad was spreading around town that I had jumped off the Winnipeg River Bridge in a suicide attempt. I couldn't believe what I was hearing. That was not the truth or even close to it. Why would he be saying that? To make me look mentally unstable?

I started wondering if he'd stepped on my fingers when I was hanging off the bridge. Was I imagining that? Why didn't he try to grab my hands, instead of just looking at me? Did he want me to fall to my death? That would fulfill his plans; he would get rid of me and say I committed suicide because I was a nut case. After all, wasn't that what he was telling everyone? I was "crazy".

A few months later, we were having another argument about our relationship. Again, he had come home after being away for a number of days. I had no doubt he was now sleeping with another woman. He grabbed a pair of scissors and held them to my throat, saying he was going to kill me and then kill himself! I numbed out again, and he removed them from my neck. In cold anger, I threw a plate of spaghetti at him. It missed him, and created an expressionistic painting on the cedar wall! He took off again, and this time he said he wasn't coming back. I hoped he meant it this time. He seemed to have a lot of places to stay.

This was getting too scary for me, so instead of taking the chance of him coming back and making another attempt on my life, I took off for Ontario to see my brother and spend a week with him. I guess I was escaping in a way. I told no one. I just took off and planned not to go home again, anytime soon. That was a bad mistake. Things happened. When I got back and called my best friend, she told me that my father had phoned, as my mother was hospitalized and he'd tried to call me. He was very worried, as no one knew where I was. He was crying on the phone and asking my friend to find me, as knowing I was okay would his birthday present. I felt so bad. At the same time, I received another phone call from Laurel's father. She had also been hospitalized with a serious, life-threatening injury after being kicked in the stomach by a racehorse at the Winnipeg Racetrack where she worked. She was asking for me. We had become close friends, and I could never blame her for what my husband had done. She was only a child, he was an adult. I was terribly alarmed and took off for Winnipeg to see my foster daughter in the hospital. After that, I headed to Swan River to see my parents. This was summer, the last summer before my father passed away.

I realized there was no escape from the nightmare my life had turned into, or from this man. I was in a prison in my mind. I had to stay home, and he would show up whenever he felt like it and take off whenever he felt like it, staying away as long as he wanted to and doing whatever pleased him. I had to bite the bullet and not let fear make me do things that would hurt those I loved. I was in a trap, a tangled web, and I didn't know how to get out. I was always afraid of being alone, like in the dreams. I never wanted to be alone. My parents needed to be looked after, while my marriage was falling apart, and my life was dangling from a thin thread. I wasn't wanted; I was not worth anything to the man I once loved and married. He wanted me dead! Why? Greed? I felt so worthless; I just wanted to die. But I couldn't even do that, as my parents were still alive and needed me. I was worth a great deal to my loving father, and my mother also needed me, but she had my father to look after her. He had no one but me.

Is it worth it?

That was the question I began to ask myself. Was this kind of life, with all its heartache and pain, worth living? Did I deserve to live? I knew nothing of post-traumatic stress, but the feeling of worthlessness was starting to take me down a slippery, dark slope to a bottomless pit. He didn't want me, so I was better off leaving this world. I was such a pitiful victim. I was still trying to please this man, just like I had always tried to please my mother and get her approval and love. This had become my makeup and my pattern.

The cheating, lying and neglect were getting worse, and the attempts on my life were becoming more obvious. I'd already taken the school year off and didn't even think of seeking disability. I just wanted to see if this would make things better, but it only made them worse. He spent even less time at the farm, and he thought I was spying on him, so he became all the more secretive. But by staying home, I could at least take care of the cattle, which he was not doing.

People whom I told about my marriage didn't understand. They told me to leave him, but they didn't understand how the mind of a victim works. We don't think like normal people do. Our minds have been programed by the indoctrination of our spouses. We have patterns of our own. Around 33 per cent of women will be abused by their spouses in some form, I was told by a counselor. If they weren't so victimized after their thinking was warped, the statistics wouldn't be as high. They would know what is coming, and they'd get out! They'd run for the hills. Something I should have done!

Now for his Plan B, to drive me to suicide by his "make crazy" tactics, his emotional blackmail, his indoctrination.

I was close to committing suicide, but not close enough. I would be much closer later on, as things got even worse. I turned to another survival tactic. I would make him desire me by looking good and making him jealous!

Chapter 29: The Games We Play

This urge to be attractive and to attract men was overwhelming, even if I didn't go to bed with them. The desire to play around had started earlier, while Brad was still with me and cheating on me. What was good for the gander was also good for the goose. I wanted to see what was so attractive out there that he never came home. Maybe I could do what he did. Maybe I could get even. Maybe he'd be jealous and find me attractive again, as he once must have felt to want to marry me. Maybe we could start all over and save what we had. Maybe he would understand what I felt when he was out gallivanting around if I did the same to him. Many maybes or perhaps it was just the psychological change of life that women experience, the mid-life crisis. I had heard of many women who took off with another woman's husband around the age of thirty-five. It's like trying to be a teenager again, or going back to one's youth and wanting to feel the same things. The hunt and the hunted, the meat market, the game!

All in the name of love and looking for it in all the wrong places! This was shortly after my suicide idea. If I was going to be called "crazy" I might as well act the part.

That summer of 1984, I went to pick up some of my father's tools at the farm, six kilometers away. I didn't see Brad's truck, as it was hidden behind the house. I opened the cable across the road, as I didn't think he was around. When I opened the door to the house, he quickly pushed me outside and pushed me back down the road. I smelled a woman's perfume and felt a presence in the house, in the bedroom. He kept pushing me, and I kept pushing back, wanting to get my tools and probably trying to catch him with whoever he'd brought to the house to have sex with the night before. Suddenly he grabbed my throat, and I thought, *oh, oh, this is it now. This is when I'm really going to die; he's going to choke me.* Again, he suddenly stopped, spit in my face, and said, "If I knew what to do with your ugly body, I'd kill you!" He said it again, the "kill" word. So why was I still trying to deal with him? He wanted me dead so he could get it all, everything we'd both worked for. There was no longer any doubt in my mind. That was still his Plan A. Murder! Go back to Plan A, if Plan B doesn't work, and it hadn't, as I hadn't taken my life yet, only thought about it. I was not insane enough to be admitted to the psychiatric ward, which he had been hopeful would happen.

I was going down fast. My husband living away from home and not looking after the farm meant it was being neglected, which brought me down even more. We were losing cattle by the number. We had a lot of healthy big calves die for no apparent reason. I got Brad to take one of the dead calves into the U of M for a post mortem to find the cause of death. We were losing money steadily on the farm, as he wasn't doing anything to make it work for us as a business. I could only do so much, and I knew I had to go back to work again. I had to bring home a salary or we would lose the farm.

I had no way of contacting him, as I never knew where he was. Then he came to see me one day wanting to buy a new swather. He told me that it was around $12,000. I agreed to a loan for the swather, only to find out later from the dealer that he had paid only $9,000 for it. What did he do with the extra $3,000? There were more discrepancies in the bank accounts, subtle ones that most people would miss ... that I had missed.

The neighbour at the farm, who wasn't able to handle his own finances, became another victim. Edward had Ralph look after all his banking business. When Ralph left, Brad took over. I learned later that there were many discrepancies in Edward's bank account. It looked like his social assistance and OAS were cashed after being signed by Edward but not deposited into his account. Edward was losing money constantly.

I also started to find out about secret bank accounts Brad had everywhere. I knew for sure about one in BC he got his father to open up for him and his father jointly. Ralph's new wife showed me the bank statement. Ralph's $1,000 wedding present, a cheque made out by me, was deposited into an account made out in Brad's name. Then I wondered if the $15,000 cheque I'd made out to Ralph had also gone into this secret account along with the money Brad was embezzling from me and anyone else he could deceive.

I found another account in Fort Frances, where his grandmother lived in a nursing home. When she passed away, he was able to get what little money she had left and deposit it into this account. I discovered this several years later when I searched his name in the unclaimed accounts registry. His name came up with a $400 unclaimed balance in a bank in Fort Francs that had been opened in the summer of 1984!

I was starting to see another pattern. I learned what blame passers and excuse makers abusive people can be. Men like Brad would transfer the blame to someone else. I couldn't believe my ears when he accused me of having an affair before we even had marital problems. I was faithful, and he was the only one I wanted to be with in the first ten years of our marriage. That should have been a sign, but it didn't register at the time. Later, when he accused me of having secret bank accounts, it did hit me. He was accusing me of something he was doing. He was "transferring" what he was doing to me. Soon I knew what he was doing by what he accused me of, like seeing men on the side, having secret bank accounts, being a selfish pig, not doing my job, being an abusive wife, spreading lies about him, and my wanting everything. I even found a note that read "husband abuse" by the phone, which he had left for me to see. I was the abuser; he was the victim in his eyes! Transfer!

One day, I picked up the phone bill and noticed multiple phone calls to the same number in Beausejour. I did an intensive search and found out that it belonged to a woman named Rea. By now I was becoming a good detective. I did more research and discovered that she worked in the bank in the next town as a bank teller. I went in to see her one day and asked her point-blank if Brad had been calling her. She had the eyes of an owl and gave me the dirtiest look ever; she said she knew him, and if I didn't get out of the bank, she would have me removed. I left and started to look for her address, which I could find in the phone book. I asked around about her and was told that she could be wicked if she were aroused. I wondered what he saw in her; she wasn't even pretty, but she did own property in town which would have been worth something. One day, in June of 1984, I decided to go strawberry picking early in the morning, at a farm near the next town to us. Something made me go to her house, which I had already driven by before.

His white Thunderbird, which he said he had bought with our money for me, was sitting in front of her house. There was dew on the car, and it felt cold, so I knew he had spent the night there. I walked up to her door and knocked. I heard voices inside, but no one opened the door. I wanted to let him know, that he did not need to come home anymore, he was free to leave, and live with her. I knocked again, and still, no one answered the door. The voices angered me, so acting compulsively, I kicked in the door. They both came running out at me, yelling, and she started to attack me. I had never witnessed a human "cat" fight, but I was to be exposed to one that morning. She grabbed my hair and started yanking it out. Brad quickly grabbed me from behind, pinning my arms against my body so I couldn't put them up to deflect the blows. She whacked me in the head, again pulling out hair, and she hit my cheek with the heel of her hand. I slid down, almost unconscious from the blows to my head, and fell to the ground. I saw her boot coming at my face and body, as she booted me over and over. I couldn't find my arms to defend myself. I was going out, losing consciousness.

Suddenly, I felt my self being picked up by Brad and thrown into my car like a sack of potatoes and told to go home, which I did. I was stunned for the rest of the day. Sometimes people are so intuitive and call at just the right time. My friend Delores called me and knew right away by my voice that something was wrong. I told her my story, she told me to go see a doctor and the police right away.

I went to the doctor and reported the incident to the RCMP. They asked me if I wanted to press charges against Ruth, but I said no, realizing I might be to blame because I had kicked in her door and instigated the fight. But I wanted to lay charges against my husband.

I got another phone call that proved to be intuition on someone else's part. This lady was my sponsor in Al Anon. She asked me what had happened and made arrangements for me to go to Hazelton, Minnesota, to a campus for addicts and also for spouses of addicted people. I looked at myself in the mirror and saw how awful I looked. My eye was almost swollen shut, and I had a huge black bruise above and below my left eye.

I packed and was ready to leave when Brad came home. He sat on the couch, looked me straight in the eye, and said, "She did not hit you!" I was furious. That was when I finally realized the relationship was over. ***I no longer wanted to live with this man. I was super done with him!*** I had no more love for him. I just needed to get myself together and I was going to go for divorce. Nothing would stop me now.

I spent a week recovering at the campus. It was worth the $400 I had to pay. I learned about addiction diseases, abusiveness, about how to get myself back on track again. I also realized this was for wives of addicts more than for victims of abuse. I was able to talk to some men who were walking the campus. One told me he was there because of alcohol addiction and that his work place had sent him and paid for his treatment. He told me alcoholics were locked in for one month before they were allowed to walk around the campus. Drug addicts were locked up and in treatment for six months. The meals were terrific, the campus was nice, and I was able to heal before going home again.

When I got home, I went to Casey's Inn, as I was once again the lonely, betrayed woman looking for love in the wrong place. But instead of going in, I sat outside, watching people leave and listening to some country music on the radio. It was too late to go in, I thought. All of a sudden, I saw my husband come out of the hotel with his arm around two women. They were drunk, and they were loud. One was younger and prettier, and the other one was much older, but still attractive. I confronted him and asked him to come home. It was past midnight. The older woman said, "He's coming with me, he's mine!" He went with them. The next morning, I thought, I was going to get even.

I phoned the mean-spirited Rea to let her know that he was seeing other women and not just her. I phoned around nine a.m. She wouldn't believe me, saying he had spent the night with her and left around eight o'clock that morning. I was flabbergasted. I had seen him with those two women he was going home with at around midnight, and he had gone to Beausejour to spend the rest of the night with Rea? Three women in one night? What did this mean? Did he have a different addiction? Was he a sexaholic and not an alcoholic? I let it go and concentrated on looking after the cattle. He had his new swather now, which I was using. We were still losing calves at the farm.

I resigned myself to the fact that I was just biding my time before filing for divorce, as I needed money. I would take care of everything at home because someone had to; I was always the one having to do it, anyhow. I would be the Superwoman once again, push my pain deep inside of me, and carry on as normal. There was nothing I could do anymore but wait.

I went by the farm one day on my way to old Pinawa Dam to see Howard, an elderly neighbour of ours who was nice to me and was lonely. As I was going by the farm, I saw a white calf with his legs up in the air, going through death throes. I jumped out of the car and ran over to try to save him. He was in agonizing pain and died in my arms. I couldn't stand this torture a helpless animal was going through. I had just received a letter addressed to Brad the day before, which said the calf we had taken to the University for Examination had died from battery acid poisoning. I never showed this letter to Brad, as I didn't see him much. I thought to myself that these calves that twere dying so suddenly must have gotten acid poisoning from the batteries he left lying around. I couldn't drive to the house because of the cable he had put across, so I had to walk to it. I saw inadequate one wire electric fencing that kept the cows out but not the calves. They would sneak under the wire and go for the lush grass around the farmhouse, home to all the hoarded junk the two men had acquired.

The whole place looked like a hoarder's paradise. I had tried to clean it up, but it was just too much, so I'd concentrated on keeping the house clean. I saw a couple of calves on the wrong side of the fence and then I saw the batteries lying all over the place. I picked up thirteen old batteries and put them in the back of his old truck so that the calves couldn't reach them. I knew that battery acid was something cattle would lick, as they liked the taste of it, a salty taste. I'd never heard of any calves dying after that. I got to see how cruel this man really was. The calves suffered a horrible, agonizing death, as I witnessed when I discovered this calf dying.

Things were expediting. I called Rea to let her know she could have him, as I no longer wanted him. I wanted her to tell him, not to come to the house anymore. If he was going to lie and defend a girlfriend against a wife, he didn't even have loyalty as a positive trait. He had no positive traits at all anymore; he was an evil monster, in my eyes! He would stick up for her, the wrong doer, against me! She told me that he wasn't that good in bed, and she thought I should have known that he was involved with a woman called Cindy now. I remembered her as the woman I had talked to at the trailer. He must have been living with Cindy if he wasn't coming home. But where?

I learned something very significant about abusers that summer. The girlfriends are treated so well, and the victims are treated like crap. If the abusive man, had another woman, she would be the honeymoon and I would be the blow. I wouldn't get any honeymoons anymore, which was another reason I was ready to end the relationship for good. What I had looked forward to before, was no longer happening. There were no more honeymoons. She was getting them all. If I was out of the picture, he'd need to look for another victim. This was another reason for me to get a divorce. I also started to wonder about all the loose women who got into relationships with cheating men, especially men who cheated so often with so many different women. Did they not see that if the man could cheat on the wife, he'd likely also cheat on them? I wouldn't want a man as promiscuous as Brad. Was I the only prudish woman in the country? Did all divorced and single women cheat with men? Did they have no conscience?

I had several men come to see Brad's poor, sexually deprived wife, as they would likely think of me. They brought alcohol with them and wanted to go to bed with me. I kicked them out of the house and told them to have sex with their wives and say to them the nice things they were saying to me. I couldn't stand these men wanting to cheat on their wives, as I knew only too well how devastating and hurtful that could be. Later, some men came to see me and thanked me for what I'd said, as did some wives. I had morals and principles, and cheating was morally wrong, in my books. But obviously it wasn't to these women.

I started to hate him and hate them just as much. The summer was going by and nothing changed, but things got worse for me. I was sinking into a depression and knew I had to act, but I was so naive about divorce and scared of it as well. I didn't know who to go to. And then it happened at the end of August, when I was planning to go back to work again at Powerview school.

Chapter 30: Plans B and C

I was at the farmhouse, when he came in from somewhere. He had a paper in his hand. He told me this was a "quick divorce option" for us. By me signing the paper, I would set us both free. If I loved him, I would sign it, he said. I was sick to my stomach after I read it. It would give me a divorce, and it would give him all the assets, every single thing we'd built and bought together! No half and half, as he has promised me in the past, when he got Ralph to sign over the three properties to him. Everything was to be signed over to him. There was no name of a lawyer on the paper; but it was just typed out to look official. Through the tears, I scribbled my name on the back in huge letters and told him to get out of there and leave me alone. This man did want it all, as I'd overheard him say! The greedy bastard! I hadn't even filed for a divorce at that time, so he was giving me nothing I wanted in return for all he wanted! And to use "loving him" as a tool was emotional blackmail! Once again… the guilt trip. I hated him but seemed to love him at the same time; or did I love the ten years we'd spent together that were loving and so beautiful? Did I love what no longer was and want it back?

> ***Lady, stop looking for the good in him. Start looking for the "real," as "good" is easy to fake, but real cannot be faked. You've been deceived by this man who always wore a mask. See what's behind the mask; maybe now you see it and will believe it!***

I had no idea who made up this paper or what happened to it. That was in August. After that day, he came to the home less and less. He was living with Cindy somewhere else, I guessed. I was indeed going crazy with all the "make crazy" things he was doing to me, but of course with all the "transfers," blame passing, and emotional blackmail, I was feeling guilty and that I was to blame. If you throw enough mud at the wall, some is bound to stick, and I'd had a lot of mud thrown at me. It was starting to stick! I was crazy, so I was going to act the part, and I had to do things for survival or just end it all.

One day after he'd been away for a while, I wanted to confront him. I saw him coming down River Road toward me and decided to stop him with my car. I cranked the wheel so we would meet head-on to get him to stop, but suddenly I found out that I had no brakes, so we had a head-on collision at a low speed. Why did my brakes not work? Had he tampered with them? It was bizarre, yet kind of humorous, and a touch embarrassing. "Head-on collision of husband and wife!" It would read in the local newspaper. These events led to my adding a stipulation to my will that if I died prematurely, my death should be investigated.

Another time, his truck was parked in the yard but was locked. He was always locking his truck, and so I wondered what he had to hide in it? I was very annoyed with this, so I decided to run his truck into the river! I couldn't unlock it, so I tried to push it with my car by putting something in front of my bumper so I wouldn't damage it. I pushed and pushed, but it wouldn't move. I guess the brakes were on or it was in gear. I gave up and tried something else on another day. When he came up alongside of me in his truck and on his way to see another woman, I kicked his door and left huge dent. I thought to myself, you want to think me crazy? You ain't seen nothing yet, boy! I was ready to spice his food with ex-lax or go and see all his girlfriends and tell them about the others he had, just to make them jealous. These were the "make crazy" things his cheating would make me want to do. None of them worked. They always backfired on me, so what was the point? I was now Super Insane, I thought. But I did find out why he locked the truck. One day I noticed a set of keys in a small cabin we had by the house, where he had hidden them. I took them to open the truck to see if they were the right keys. They were. I found men's deodorant, and a bottle of Apricot Brandy behind the seat. I also found a 22 rifle. When he saw I had the keys, he grabbed them away from me, and hid them again in a different place.

Then a friend of ours came to the house and told me that Brad had told him he was trying to drive me into the psychiatric hospital. Brad told him that if I were committed, he could sell any property we had, without me signing off on it. I was shocked, but when I looked it up in a law book, I discovered that it could be done. All my "act crazy" things stopped when I learned what was going through his evil mind. No wonder he had encouraged me to get my psychiatrist to sign a paper to say I was mentally incompetent and that I would be committed. The doctor had just looked at me when I put the paper in front of him and said, "Who told you to get this signed?" When I told him, he just shook his head and said, "You are not insane; there is nothing wrong with you. You just suffered some severe trauma, and you do not belong in an institution. I will not sign this." Then he tore it up and threw it into the garbage.

Plan B wasn't working for Brad either, but he would not know this. I would also never have known if our friend had not warned me. Plan C, to take me to court was next on his agenda. I wondered how he knew so much about the law, and then it hit me. He had a school friend, that was a lawyer, and since he hardly ever worked anymore, he had time to investigate, visit this lawyer and ask questions. Some crazy things just happened to us, without any effort on our part!

One night before he moved in with Cindy, we were at home, sleeping. I had my back to him, and we both woke up at the same time. He turned toward me as I turned toward him, and for some reason I threw my hand up and it connected with his nose. It wasn't intentional; it was an accident. I saw blood running all over the place and felt badly. He jumped up, got dressed, and took off. I went after him to tell him it had been an accident and I was sorry, but I couldn't catch him. He was gone for several days. A rumour started that I had hit him and he had a broken nose and two black eyes, but I never saw that, as he didn't come home for a while. My name was being smeared as a husband abuser! Once again, I was the bad one, the monster, while he, the real monster, came out as pure as the saint! Brad was such a nice man, he would never hurt his wife; if he was spending time with other women, it was because his wife was such a bitch. The poor, poor man having to live with this "crazy" woman!

Chapter 31: Why Do Men Cheat on Their Wives?

Why was he cheating on me? I asked myself this many times. I couldn't do it to him, because I loved the comfort zone of feeling good with someone I knew. Love and loyalty were so important to me. At times, when I wanted to cheat, I felt guilty as hell and couldn't go through with it. I'd look at myself in the mirror and think, *not bad*. So what did he see in the floozies he was having affairs with? Did he even know what it felt like to be cheated on? I had heard about how angry he'd been as a ten-year old when his father cheated on his terminally ill mother, whom he loved so much. He hated his father for it. So why was it wrong for his father to cheat on his mother with one other woman but all right for him to cheat on me with any woman who would have him? Such a double standard! Could he have been as programmed by his childhood experiences as I had been by mine?

When I first found out about his cheating, I felt like absolute crap. I felt there was something wrong with me, like I was ugly, no longer exciting for him, and could no longer attract the love of my life. It was traumatic, to say the least. I would see him with the other woman, knowing what love making was like for us, and wonder how he was feeling when making love with her. But then I remembered a time several years earlier when he'd come home drunk and took me out into the field with his tuck and began to make passionate love to me. I thought, Wow, he still loves me. This is so good. But then he couldn't get it up; he went all limp, and that was the end of the anticipation of a good night of passionate love making. A friend who told me not to be depressed but think of him and his mistress as two drunks rolling around in the bed and not really feeling anything for each other.

But the thought of him making love to other women made me sick to my stomach, and I couldn't get the thoughts out of my head. When he bought the white Thunderbird and put on his leather jacket, smelling sexy with his cologne and jangling the keys to let me know he was taking off, I wanted to kill someone, anyone, but most likely him. I was his wife, but he made it very clear he was going out to "snag" a woman, and I was to stay home alone and cry my eyes out. I would get so jealous. Did he not have any feelings anymore, any conscience, any heart, or any soul? It was like living in hell, in a prison of adultery. He was so cocky as to leave with a smile on his face, and at times he even remarked that he was looking after his love life, and it was not with me! He often made it sound like a race, and the other women were ahead of me, but sometimes I was even with them.

If you're going to kill him, do it now. It would be a crime of passion, so do it now! The jail term isn't long. Catch him in bed with his floozie and kill him! Kill them both!

But this I could not do! I had spent my life rescuing and taking care of others, giving them life, saving them from death. I was constructive and could never be destructive; I couldn't even kill myself, but there were many times, I wanted to. Murder was not my thing. I was never programmed that way.

I wanted to get even, and because this caused me to lose so much weight, I was looking good: slim and trim and fun to be with. I started doing my hair up differently, piled on the makeup, wore skin-tight blue jeans and cowboy boots, and started to paint the town red. I didn't go alone. I went with my foster daughter, and we were each other's guardians. We'd dance up a storm and let guys buy us drinks and try to pick us up. The good part was that my husband was there too and would see me looking this good and popular. Maybe he'd be jealous and want to be with me too. But this didn't stop him; he was after every woman who showed any interest in him. He reminded me of a goose, his head straining in all directions to see what he could pick up that night. What was good for the gander was good for the goose, I thought, but when it came to going home with strange men, I drew the line; I just couldn't do it! I could not be like him. Two wrongs never make a right!

The games people play! You're just playing a mind game. No one ever wins in these games, and they become a vicious cycle. You're giving him an excuse to cheat on you! And you will look as bad as he does. Where is your dignity and pride? Don't sink as low as he has; he wants this! He wants you to play this game with him so you'll look as bad.

Thoughts of all his philandering kept coming back into my head. At one point, I started seeing him with the same woman a number of times and tried to find out who she was. I worked in the next town, and one day I saw him in that town as I was going to pick up some groceries at a corner store, during my lunch hour. So, I rolled down my car window to talk to him. It was lunch time, so he quickly said he'd come to take me out for lunch, but I noticed that he ate very little. A few days later, I wore my locket with our picture in it. One of my students wanted to see what was in it, so I opened it and showed it to her. She quickly piped up and said, "I know this man; he sleeps with my mom all the time!" I almost fainted! I found out this woman lived just down the road from my school, as I had taken her daughter home a few times after school. When I saw her mother, I recognized her as the one he'd been flirting with in the bar! He was actually sleeping with a woman a block away from where I worked, fifty kilometers from our home. It was so bizarre. Did my students know this? How embarrassing! He was going to drive me insane; I knew it. Plan B, since Plan A hadn't worked so far. He could switch back and forth on these plans and the end result will be the same. Everything we owned would be his. I would have spent thirteen years working on the farm and investing every cent I originally had and made working, into the farm, our home, and our relationship for nothing. He would own it all.

Wake up and smell the roses. Do you not see what he's doing? He knows he's hurting you with his cheating, so why do you think he's doing this over and over. Could it be to drive you to the edge and over it? To drive you insane? You're slipping and he's in his glory! He is the one in control here; he is controlling you! Like a robot! You are his victim!

Plan B, to drive me into an institution, was continuously in progress. With some of our valuable river frontage property in both names, he'd be able to sell it off without my signing. Better still, he could drive me to suicide. That was the best plan, a murder that wouldn't be regarded as a murder. I would be out of his life for good. But that didn't work, as I kept chickening out. So there was no choice left for Brad but to go to Plan C, the court route. He told a good friend of ours, "I'm going to take that bitch to court until she doesn't have a nickel to her name." I was penniless at the time. In February of 1985, he'd sold our entire herd of cattle, a farm, and equipment, so he had money to take me to court and still have enough cash left that he wouldn't have to work for six years. This gave him ample time to plan how to get rid of me. This was now plan C: a divorce and property settlement. All was in his favor.

In September 1984, after I had gone back to work, I received the regular petition for divorce and property settlement, still asking for everything because, as the bottom line said, he had acquired everything by his own work and investment. What a crock! I saw red and swore I wouldn't let him get away with it. I would fight back with all I had. Then I suddenly realized I didn't have much in the lines of ready cash. I had just put everything into the farm and had paid the last debt, leaving me broke. He planned all this very well, striking when I was in a vulnerable position, and he had no debts left to pay. I had done all this for him. I was a total sucker not to see this coming. I knew this would cost us both, but I did not anticipate the sale of the cattle, and other assets coming which enabled him to be able to pay for legal costs. I thought this divorce could be settled soon. But we were not on the same page. Once again, I was far too trusting.

He ended up taking me to court for twelve years, and he left me struggling financially. I couldn't get loans, as our assets were all in dispute. I had to work day and night, two jobs. I made crafts to sell; sold milk from the cows I had bought after we separated, and even raised chickens to sell. I didn't have a life. I was broke and couldn't believe that a man and his new woman could be so cruel, selfish, and cold. She told me once that what Brad had was also hers, but that shouldn't have included my share of it. I went to the bank to see about our joint account and found out Brad had closed it and taken all the money out of it. He had just sold a piece of property to our neighbour to widen a road running through our property and had received $10,000 for it, but I got nothing. The neighbours thought he would give me my share of the money, but Brad never did.

I had to quickly find a lawyer to defend me, but was clueless about all of this, as I hadn't done any research. One day Brad called me and said he wanted the furniture in the house. I was angry and totally stressed out when he brought the horse trailer and removed all that was easily movable. The last item he was going to remove was my brass bed that I had spent so many hours refinishing and polishing. I saw red again! He was even going to take our bed. Where would I sleep? He came out with the brass bar, a section of the bed. I grabbed him by the collar and then he hit me on the head three times with the brass bar. It was fortunate that the neighbour drove into the yard just then and saw him do this.

I had a witness for the first time! This was helpful later when physical abuse became a criminal offence and he was charged with assault. He even took the meat out of the freezer. He told people later that "the bitch isn't going to get the meat from one of my cows I "butchered". His cow? The offspring of one of the heifers I had bought years earlier suddenly was his cow, not our cow? The worst news came to me when he called me one day and said, he was going to pick up the horses, I had raised and worked with. He told me, he would take them to the stock market while I was working. He had already taken our entire cattle herd, so how could I stop him from loading up my horses when I was away at work? He ended the phone call by calling me "a greedy pig." *Transfer again,* I thought. He was the greedy one.

I became ill, because the horses, like the cows, were of sentimental value to me. I knew them all by name and had worked with them, trained them, looked after them, taught riding lessons on them to kids, and had used them on trail rides. They were my family. Since he had sold the whole herd of cattle, around 120 head, one day while I was at work, I didn't doubt him when he said the horses were next. I quickly borrowed a horse trailer, since he had mine at the farm, and moved my horses to other places, where I had to pay for their board. They were safe there and wouldn't be picked up when I was away at work. It was hard for me to work with them, as I had to go to different places to train them. All of this had been well planned out years in advance, and Brad's brain was constantly scheming how he could get the best of me in order to also hurt me. Abuse of a victim never stops. There are many ways to hurt someone, and he was doing a super job. He wasn't working, so he had time to plan and scheme and get ideas from others. Once we established that he could not sell the horses, I was able to bring them back. Then he started ploughing up the hay field they were on. This would mean my horses would have no grass to eat during the summer. This time I called my lawyer instantly, and had a court injunction placed against him so he would have to stop this.

Evil people with too much time on their hands can come up with some very evil schemes.

Chapter 32: Life in Danger

It's interesting how much effort an abusive person puts into hurting others and the times he picks to do it. The week before Christmas, 1984, Brad came to the house. I let him in and he told me he wanted me to move out of the house, as the woman he was living with was pregnant with his baby. My first thoughts were, *is he going to blame me for this too? I wasn't standing over their bed with a stick telling him to get her pregnant.* Then he said: it was my fault, as I had kicked him out of the house. Another lie! He'd left on his own accord and had kept me in the dark as to where he was living. I just knew who he was living with. She already had two teenage children with her ex-husband.

Then suddenly my neighbor who had bought the road allowance for $10 000 came to the house while Brad was there to ask if I had gotten half of the money from Brad. I told him no! He was a big man, so he walked over to Brad, grabbed him by the neck, and yelled at him. He actually lifted him off the floor! I couldn't help smiling. Then the neighbor left, and Brad again asked me to move. I told him to get out of the house and out of my sight. He left. This is my Christmas present, I thought, being told this to make me feel bad, as I can't conceive children. I was hurting badly enough over this … I didn't need it rubbed in my face that he wasn't the infertile one, but I was. I cried all Christmas break whenever I was not at the personal care home, visiting my mother.

It was quiet for a month, and then on Valentine's Day, 1985 I came home from school to see red flags on posts in front of my house. They were in the square shape of a house or a building of some sort. The next day, I was served a court paper asking for my house or to put another house in front of my house, which meant he was going to live next to me with his new wife and baby. I had to go to court if I didn't agree with it. He wanted to move his wife and expected baby, into my house, and I could go and live in Powerview, where I worked. He'd look after my horses and the place.

At the court session, the judge looked at him and reamed him out sternly. He said that I had proven I could look after the horses myself, and that there was no way Brad was going to move his new woman into the house when he was the one who had moved out of it and in with her. Brad's alternative plan to put a house in front of my house, between me and the river was also crushed by the judge. The third option was for his woman and him to move her cottage to the other farm that I had bought years ago and to move there, which they did. They would be by a river channel, which had a beautiful view. That suited me just fine, as it was six kilometers away from me.

Before the court day, I was having anxiety attacks just thinking of seeing him and his wife and baby right next to my house, practically in my yard. This was not a friendly parting, to say the least. So this was the valentine he had sent me: the red flags staking out the place where he was planning to put "their" house. This was so inconsiderate and cruel!

Even though the legal divorce and property settlement matters were in progress, and he was living with Cindy, I was still not out of danger as long as the court case was in progress. No one knew how it would end. But we both knew it would be costly. I kept defending myself, as it was a matter of principle and fairness. He was unfair, cruel, and selfish, and in the end, this cost him much more than he ever anticipated. It ended up costing me $150,000 over the next twelve years.

One day a very abusive cousin of Brad's showed up on my doorstep. He came with a sleazy looking friend. This cousin hadn't had a driver's license for years, and now suddenly he had one, so I saw him for the first time in around ten years. He lived thirty minutes from where I lived, but I couldn't stand the way he treated his mother. I hated being anywhere near this man who reeked of such evil. He was a drug addict and an alcoholic who viciously abused his mother. I was surprised to see him coming to visit me, as Brad was no longer living at our log house. This man had also spent time in jail, but I did not know what for.

He told me he knew I needed some work done on my house and would do it for me for $500. I did need the work done, as the hole that was made at the time of the fire four years earlier had never been filled, and it looked unsightly. I gave them the go ahead. They came and did the job, but I kept thinking of the $500. This specific amount raised a red flag. Brad once said, "It only costs $500 to get rid of a person." I found it strange that they had asked for this exact same figure. Were they there to get rid of me? Had Brad secretly hired them? I was terrified. I stayed away until they quit working for the day. When they were ready to go, I gave them $700 cash and they took off happy. They had their drug and alcohol money! Did I spoil Brad's plan by giving them, cash and more than he might have offered? My husband was always cheap and would try to whittle this cost down. Did I just save my life? I wondered why I had fallen for it in the first place. A month later, I heard a rumor that these two men had been charged with possession of drugs and liquor as they tried to cross the border in order to bring back cheap liquor. That meant that Brad's cousin would lose his driver's license again, and thus I never saw him or his friend again after they left my house.

What a fool I was, what a bloody fool, a Super Fool.

After that I felt even less safe than before, as the court case was dragging out on purpose. He would never settle; even his own lawyer was ticked off with him. I guess twelve years later he finally ran out of money, because he made an offer to let me have my house and lot while he got everything else, and did not have to pay me half of the assets he had sold. It was totally unfair, but I took it. The battle was over … finally. The black cloud was lifted, but things were still not over. There was more to come. An abuser can never let go of his victim. When all other avenues to abuse someone are closed to him, he'll find a new one, including the legal system. He wanted it all, and when he didn't get his way, vengeance set in. He was going to try to hurt me any way he could, and he did.

Chapter 33: Coming to Terms with God!

By the time we were a year into the court battle, I was hard up for money. *No* bank would lend me money when our assets were in dispute in the courts. I finally was able to borrow $5,000 to buy some equipment I needed to replace and to pay some bills. For that, I had to pay 15 per cent interest. When my mother passed away, I got another settlement of $10,000, with the house to be sold later and kept as a rental unit until then. This all went to paying lawyers. It was depressing. I also decided to pay back the monies I'd taken out of my teacher's retirement fund so I could retire at fifty-five or sixty. They wanted $30,000. Yikes! This was killing me. I got stressed out trying to make money to pay for all these extra expenses, along with living expenses. The stress seemed to cause my mystery disease to flare up, and the migraines started their marathons again. The time between migraines got to be shorter and shorter. I was in such excruciating pain that I once walked to the Winnipeg River Bridge and wondered if that was the answer to stop the pain. As I looked down, thoughts of the water swirling over my head and covering my face brought back the thoughts of incidents of the past which never stopped haunting me.

Night with no air,
My face covered
I could not breathe,
I needed air,
Air, no air!
I needed air!

I couldn't do it. I knew then that I was claustrophobic, and this likely started the day I had a pillow over my face and the arm on my neck. I shuddered and walked home in the dark. After that I would get reoccurring dreams of being trapped in tunnels, not being able to go back or forth, and the claustrophobic feeling would cause me to wake up screaming and gasping for air. Why was God allowing me to suffer so much and for so long?

Chapter 34: The Last Attempt

There comes a time in all of our lives when the mental or physical pain gets to be too much for us to take. For me, it was both. My body was wracked with pain. I spent a week in bed, hoping the severe pain in my lower back and left hip would go away, but this didn't work. The hip that was hurting was the hip that was fractured when I fell off the bridge and onto the ice. I guessed that I had arthritis in that hip. My mental pain was unbearable as well, and I had already heard enough from counsellors to know that it would be the same advice over and over, so it was pointless going to them. I had sleeping pills, but they were no longer effective. I was running out of options. The psychiatric hospital wouldn't take me, as, according to the doctor, I wasn't insane. I was just going through trauma and had an emotional breakdown. The mental stress likely had a bearing on the physical pain, as well. The world became blacker and blacker with each day. I was exhausted but couldn't sleep. I was hungry but couldn't eat. It was summer holidays, so thankfully I didn't need to go to work. I took myself off the pills, as I didn't want to take anti-depressants the doctor had prescribed. They were playing havoc with my stomach and giving me severe heartburn. I was determined to get better on my own, and if not, I had the alternative to end all the pain. I knew what I would do, which goes back to another time when I had wanted to do it but was too chicken.

But this wasn't the only motive for my next move. I was still carrying the feeling of guilt that I had done something to ruin our relationship; after all, I was being blamed for it. Deep down inside, I felt I still loved Brad, in spite of what he'd done. I believed there was a good person in him but something had messed him up. The excuse-making set in. I can only guess this is the grief one feels when losing someone they've lived with for many years and some of those years were very happy. A counsellor once told me that I was going through the grief not so much because of losing him but losing what we could have and should have had. And, of course, I wanted to make him happy. I wanted to see the good in him, not the "real." Like with my mother, I was still seeking approval by trying to please.

Getting rid of me would make him happy, and you can do this for him. Why not? You are always doing the dance for approval, trying to buy his love! You think if you give up the most precious thing you have, for him, he will love you! Give up your life? Heaven is a better place than the hell you're living in, and besides, you'll please him. So when you're gone, he'll love you for doing this! The ultimate sacrifice ... your life! For him!

My thinking went back to my childhood, trying to get the approval from someone I loved! It was time to do something! I lay awake that night planning my own demise. It was very strange, as I did it calmly and with no emotion ... just methodically planned my death in such a way that it would appear accidental so he would get my insurance policy and everything he wanted, and then he'd be happy and perhaps miss me, And love me? This was the price I was willing to pay for love, for approval. Superwoman didn't have a Super Brain. It was foolish and unacceptable; it was murder of a different sort. The murder of the child within that was suffering so much, and I knew no other way to help this child other than to take way the pain by ending this life.

This wasn't really suicide; this was murder, coldly planned murder with intent, with mens rea, murdering the child within, intentionally planned by me! And my motive was to please someone who would never appreciate it.

I had a plan, but with one hitch. I was planning to take a huge overdose of the meds I was on, like a whole bottle which was around 100 pills. But I might not die. Then this would affect Brad getting my insurance. I could suffer because of this, and suffering wasn't what I had in mind. I was already suffering enough. I didn't want to be a vegetable and burden others having to look after me. But this would be suicide, so to adhere to Plan B, I would drive my car into a huge brick wall in the city and make sure I would die. And if I didn't? That was another worry; I couldn't let myself think about it. I didn't wish to be disabled for life with no one wanting to look after me. I had to think this over carefully. To carry out my original plan, I went to the old Pinawa Dam, a place I loved so much. It was always a good place to think, with the rugged beauty around me. The water was rushing by me, and I could feel the smooth rocks, visualize the rugged, wild beauty of nature, as I sat there with my eyes closed. I sat there for a long time contemplating the pros and the cons, in cold blood, calmly, methodically. Planning how to do it! There were no emotions left, and this made it serious. I was going to do this, and nothing would be able to stop me. But something more powerful than anything else came to my rescue, the power of the Creator.

The sky was clouded over, and rain was expected. I went down on my knees, wanting to pray, and suddenly something hit me: God did not care. God allowed this pain; God allowed my husband to become this cruel, uncaring, and cold-blooded man. God was supposed to sanction this union of marriage. Why was he allowing it to be torn apart?

Until death us do part!

I became very angry! I looked up to the heavens and hated God, screaming up to the sky, "THERE IS NO GOD" as loud as my voice could shout. I did this again, and then suddenly, like a torrent of water beside me, the tears came streaming down my cheeks, and I bowed my head and prayed to God to forgive me for what I had just said.

Something turned my life around that day.

My plans to take my life ended with that prayer. The answer to my pain wasn't to take my life to make this man happy and rich; it was to let God carry me and my burden for a while until I was able to carry it again by myself. He did, but at the time I got to realize what a Super Fool I had just been.

You fool; you were going along with Brad's master plan to get rid of you. You were making this happen for him. Stop this and think. Do you not see what he was doing to you, and how you were buying into his plan for you, and making it work for him? This is what he wants! To get everything and get you out of the way for good!

Don't do it!

This wasn't the way; this was not the answer. God spoke to me that day: "This is not the way." I had to find another way. I made many phone calls to seek for proper counselling, and through these many calls came an answer: EVOLVE.

I discovered EVOLVE[14] after Brad had already moved out and was living with her and her baby-on-the-way, a baby I couldn't conceive. I needed to find out what had happened in this marriage that seemed to have been made in heaven fifteen years earlier but had turned into hell. I found out in the EVOLVE meetings that I'd been abused by him verbally and psychologically, and towards the end it had progressed to physical and sexual abuse. The most subtle and perhaps worst type of abuse was triggered by the greed, the obsession of wanting money and possessions, wanting it all. He financially used me for fifteen years. He had broken me financially by letting me be the one to pay down the debts and support him. Then when the time was right for him, he wanted it all and tried to get rid of me with his three schemes: Plans A, B, and C. I was the Super Fool enough to take care of everything, even paying for everything. When the final offer was made, I was to get the house and lot I was on, but no cash for the assets he sold without my approval. He was to get ten times more in assets than I was, and I was the one who had originally paid for them all.

It was time to get out before I lost my life, as so many women do. I found out that I had a lot in common with all the other women in my group therapy sessions at EVOLVE. The patterns of abusiveness were mostly the same, and abuse didn't discriminate. I needed to understand and come to

---

14   EVOLVE offers counselling for women experiencing domestic violence. See appendix.

terms with all I had gone through and figure out why I was such a victim. I was told to look within myself and then at my roots. With the guidance of two very good counsellors, I found the answers.

Unfortunately, they came a little too late, and I was not unscathed. The scars will be with me forever, and so will the memories haunt me in regards to all the ugliness that transpired. The trauma I suffered led to severe post-traumatic stress, and in the distant future, I would still feel the pillow over my head, the scissors to my throat, and smell death when something would trigger it off. I tried to put these away in a box and only looked at them when I didn't understand where I was at and where I was going. Would I ever deal with all of this? I doubt that a lifetime is long enough, but I would try. I would try.

Chapter 35: How Abuse Works

Being verbally, emotionally, and financially abused is to live a life of torture, and it often becomes unbearable. Death becomes an option, as death will end it, death of the perpetrator or the victim. This gave a whole new perspective to "'til death do us part." Was this the answer? To get rid of him, and the pain. I read the book, *The Burning Bed* and could so identify with the woman in it. I also watched the movie *The Color Purple* and cried through the whole movie. At the part where, Whoopi Goldberg, the victim in the movie holds a razor blade to her abusive husband's neck as she's shaving him, and hesitates for a brief moment. I knew exactly what was going through her head. But the moment passed, and it didn't end there.

The moments when I wanted to kill myself to end it all were also brief moments in time, but I couldn't do it. I couldn't kill anything or anyone, and I was a person too. But until death us do part, the abuse would never stop, even after parting. Neither would the fear and anxiety of being a victim go away as long as the abuser was still living and could figure out something to do to hurt me.

I had spent five years in a living hell. Constant cheating by my husband and the humiliation it caused me almost broke me. He neglected the bills and the farm. He left me lonely during long nights at home, with only my thoughts and my heartache. I was living in a prison of prisons and couldn't find the key to let myself out. I cried constantly when I was alone, and sometimes I couldn't hold the tears back in company either. I became self-isolated, not wanting to share my pain with others or make them feel uncomfortable. I was too ashamed to tell anyone what I was going through. I needed love so badly but had none. I needed support but there was none. I became a loner, a hermit, and sought relief in gardening and writing. I needed to see some justice done; I needed to see the abuser suffer too and know that he had to deal with the consequences of what he'd done to me. But this never happened, and likely never would, in my lifetime. Why was I the only one to suffer when I'd run into him and her so often in a small town? Every time his new woman saw me, she had a smug look on her face, which turned into a smirk instead of a smile. A smirk is a smile on someone's face when they don't look at you but you know it was meant for you to be humiliated and demeaned.

And the manipulations continued. Brad told men to come and see me because I was good in bed. One man admitted this to me. Was this so Brad could catch me in bed with one and have an excuse for a divorce? Who would sell their own wife to another man? Who could sink so low? But then again, who could get a teenage foster daughter drunk and have men come and visit her for sex while he watched? As the two young men had once told me! This was so cold, and I often wondered if t this was really true. They seemed to have a purpose, but why did they really do this? It wasn't something you told a wife unless it was a sinister warning! Sometimes the truth hurts so much we just want to curl up and cry as a means of running away. But one has to face the truth to deal with it; running away never works. Only the truth can truly set us free. I had to face it: my husband was a cold-hearted man who would do anything for money and would even resort to crime, if he thought he could get away with it. He was a predator, while I was his prey to play with like a fox plays with a mouse, it catches and intends to kill and eat after torturing it.

I didn't want men to come and see me, but they were coming almost daily. I turned them all away. One man would sneak up on me and try to sexually assault me. I had to fight him off constantly. He was a relative to my husband, was he being sent on purpose? One time while fighting him off I saw a sharp knife on the table and was tempted to use it on him, to hurt him like he was hurting me. Finally, when I threatened police action, he backed off and left me alone. Another man felt I should be his new woman, as I was now single again, and the stalking that came out of this lasted for half a year. I wanted to hide from them all, as some wouldn't take a "no" or listen to any protests. They were persistent. I was ignorant at the time but later realized they were on drugs. I knew so little about this.

I'd hear cars come down the road and would hide under the bed or in closets like I'd done in the past. Would this fear never end? One time I ran to hide behind a tool shed. The man walked to the house to knock on my door, and my friendly dogs brought him straight to me. I lived in constant fear, not only of my husband but because of the fear of sexual assault based on the implication that I wanted sex and should have sex with these men. I was still married, and in my books, that didn't allow for sex with men other than my husband. I was not a flirt or a whore, and I didn't want to have sex with these men, some of whom were married to women I knew well. I wasn't that desperate, although they seemed to think I should be. It made me feel so cheap. Life to me was a maze, not knowing which way to turn to get out of it. Could I lay charges? No, as it was hard to pinpoint the truth, and the police at that time always said they didn't get mixed up in domestic disputes. These were only sexual assault attempts, so it was my word against theirs, with no evidence to back up my allegations.

I wanted to hurt him back and tried to figure out ways to do this, but it wasn't my forte, and what I did always backfired on me, so I gave up on that too. I was living in a hell, even after splitting up, and didn't know how to get out of this situation. I couldn't do the things he did to survive this hellish relationship. I had no power over him, but he still controlled me. Before we split up, I was in a position of weakness while he kept me in line, because I was bound to marriage vows. He was not; he didn't even go to church or believe n God. After leaving me, he used the legal process to stress me out totally, and he could get away with it as long as he had the bucks to do it, and he did. Another way of controlling and punishing me was spreading false and malicious rumors about me in the community. One of them was that I was stalking him and his family. Would I be foolish enough to stalk a man who still had motive to kill me? I could just imagine what he would do, as I knew he always kept a rifle by the door. I could just visualize it, him shooting me and then claiming this was an accident, he thought there was a bear near his house. This was humorous! Another one, I also found humorous, was when he told me that he caught me spying on his place with binoculars, from across the river. I had no idea how to get to the other side of the Pinawa

Channel, and besides, he had taken everything from the house, including the binoculars I used to have. But sadly enough there is no way of defending oneself against rumors.

I wanted to talk, to strike back at him with words, to make him feel guilty, but this would not work either as he would call the police and say I was harassing him and his family. Words were twisted, and I was accused of being the one at fault for our marriage breakdown. I felt guilty because I'd get angry and yell at him. I was afraid I was becoming a different person, and I was starting to feel out of control and very depressed. Like clay, I had been molded into someone I was not. And then one day I would become a rock.

He was always looking to get an inheritance. Money that he didn't have to work for was important to him. Shafting people and stealing from them was his obsession. His theory was that there was a sucker born every day, and they were to be taken advantage of. He could always find more suckers, as the world is full of women like me who are easy prey. Men like this will suck it all up, and they're never pleased with or appreciate what we "suckers" do for them. But we're not really suckers; we're just good, gentle souls who, because or our own honesty and integrity, aren't equipped with the armor of defense we really need, so we're vulnerable. These narcissistic men know how to feed on this vulnerability, and we become easy targets. They're the parasites and we're the hosts. They're the predators and we're the prey. They will suck us dry and then be put out when we have no more to give. They'll blame us for any problem that arises because they never take responsibility for what they do to damage a relationship. They won't try to make the relationship work, because that would be admitting that they share some of the responsibility. And they can always find new hosts to prey on. They are sick people with Narcissistic Personality Disorders (NPD). They feel entitled to what they steal or take away.

NPD progresses with age and won't stop until the person seeks professional help, but the very nature of the disease prevents them from doing this. They always have to be right, and their superegos make them think that they have done no wrong. Only the rest of the world is at fault, never them. Those of us who are uneducated about this and naive are always hoping things will get better, but the chances of that happening are slim. Instead of fueling their fires, we just need to get out and run for the hills before we get hooked into these relationships. We're told we're stupid to stay in these relationships by those who have never experienced one. We're asked why we put up with it. We ask ourselves this later, and even beat ourselves up for our ignorance. It is then that we need to take a good look at ourselves and ask why we act this way, so we can deal with it and make necessary changes in our way of thinking. This is hard but not impossible. One counselor told me, to look at myself in the mirror and tell that person, in the mirror, at least once a day, "you are a good person". I did this for years, it worked. I got to see my worth, and found wonderful friends, who loved me and would support me, once I stopped beating myself up, for what I never did in the first place.

If we stop and think, we realize we never chose these men, but they chose us, and we were too taken in by their hooks to say, no! They are con men who take advantage of us and choose us for a reason. We are professionals. We have integrity and honour, and we are caring people. Because of our honesty, we can't believe that others are dishonest. The abusers, being dishonest, never really trust us and watch us like hawks, using their control devices that work so well on us. They do not trust us as they know they are not trustworthy themselves. They are charming to being with, so we think we made the right choice in allowing them into our lives, our homes, our hearts, and our beds.

In trying to figure things out, I often came up with theories, to explain what was going on in my life. I had heard so many times from ignorant people that it takes two to cause a marriage to fail. Well, in some cases it does, but I don't agree with this. Yes, it takes two to make a marriage, but it only takes one to rip it apart. In my case, Brad wanted it to end because he had another host in mind after draining me; a host who had more to offer as he had already drained me financially. Obviously there was money involved. He didn't go for counselling or do anything to make our relationship work. He wanted it fail, but just in case things didn't work out, he also wanted a backup plan.

One day the truth came out in a foolish request he made. This was before his divorce papers were served on me. He came to the house and told me that we had a good relationship but now he wanted to "play house with another woman." Not that he'd fallen in love with someone else and out of love with me, but he "wanted to play house with someone else."

I should have asked if she had money.

Then he went on to say, "But sex was always good for us. I'd like to come and visit you sometimes, and if this new woman doesn't work out, I'd like to come back!" That again was keeping me on his leash, just in case. This was a good example of wanting control and wanting the best of both worlds.

I replied, "Over my dead body!" I realized later that wasn't the best thing to say under those circumstances when he had motive to kill me! One can laugh about these things now. Words and clichés can have double meanings! Humor is the best medicne when in pain.

I didn't have any money left. I had worked hard and put everything I had into paying the last debt we had on the farm. We were in the clear and had a nice accumulation of assets. We were going to be fine and would have been comfortably rich someday. This was good time for a con artist to strike if he had another prospect in mind, but at the same time very foolish, as by doing this he lost far more than he ever gained. By selling off some of our assets he was in a position of strength. He wanted all that we had accumulated and that I had invested in and worked so hard for, and also what he could get from his new woman. In other words, he wanted it all! He indeed was the greedy person. I would often think of his words I overheard one night, "What do I do to get rid of her? Shoot her? I admit I'm a greedy SOB." That may have been one of the few truths he ever told. He definitely was greedy.

In summer of 1983, after he mentioned playing house with another woman, he had the audacity to come to the house, once again, all smiles and charm, to ask me for $10,000 to buy a trailer for the another parcel of land we had on the Lee River Channel, saying we could move there and sell the place we were living in. He said he wanted us to start over again. That sounded good but he had already told me he wanted to play house with another woman. So I was wary. Red flags suddenly went up. I was about to receive $10,000 from my father before my father passed away in January of 1984, and Brad must have found out about that in order to come up with that specific figure. The only way I could see how he found out, was that he was outside of my open window in the house at night, listening to me talking on the phone. I remembered hearing someone running outside and getting into a vehicle and driving off. I had never told him about this gift from my father. Sure, I thought, *move me to the other farm, into a trailer I'm going to pay for, and then sell the land and take the money, as it's in your name.*

It had been a bad mistake to put the land in his name only when Brad had his father transfer the properties he owned. This sounded pretty fishy to me, but Brad had promised me half if we ever split up. I was not to find out how this would compromise my legal defense to his divorce and property settlement claim until in the future. If it was in his name only, it had to be his! Then I made a call to inquire about the trailer he was talking about and learned it was only $6,500 not $10,000. I was onto him and his schemes. He even hugged me that day and acted as though he still loved me when he asked for the money! Then he left again, angry that he didn't get his way, because I said no! I was finally starting to see the man behind the mask. But why did it take so long? Too much damage had already been done, and I still didn't want to believe he could do these kinds of things to me. Those five years, starting in 1980, were a very rough and dangerous roller coaster ride for me.

When he had mentioned that he might want to come back to me if "playing house with another woman" didn't work, I added to my first retort, "You move in with another woman, and that is it for us. "There will never be a 'going back,' and because of the cheating and the lying, the stealing, the betrayal, there won't even be a chance of a friendship." I finally started to put my foot down. It felt good!

This was all too hurtful and unnecessary. I started to realize the women he was chasing were no better than I was, and we did have something so good at one time. To give this up because of greed was not a good reason at all. We had a good future now that all the bills had been paid. We could be millionaires someday if we kept on going the way we had been, with both of us working and accumulating farm assets. In fourteen years, I had managed to pay off $40,000 worth of debts, buy twelve heifers for a basic herd as well as all the new machinery we needed. I also bought three parcels of land to add to what we already had We had four parcels of land that would someday be worth a great deal. Added to this were the three parcels of land I had bought, one had river frontage on the Lee River Channel. We were in good standing and about to adopt children, and maybe that would make it possible to have children of our own. In Vitro Fertilization was an option, and with the debts paid, we could have paid for it.

On top of all this, we were still young and healthy and had wonderful friends. To toss all of it away so recklessly for greed was foolish, and to try to manipulate me after all the cheating, was also foolish. It made for a bad parting, future hatred, and lack of trust. I knew that I never wanted to see or talk to this man again, a man I had slept with and loved for ten out of fifteen years, we lived together. I felt like I'd been "sleeping with the enemy" instead of a man I loved for the last five years. I heard this was a title of a movie, and thus wanted to see it. The man behind the mask was showing his "real" face. What he lacked in intelligence was made up for by his cunning, and women like me are far too trusting and thus easily fooled and betrayed.

Sometimes a soft note would hit me and I wondered, because of the look in his eyes, if he were on drugs, smoking weed or drinking. Maybe this had changed him. I'd heard there was some bad stuff, like LSD, being sold on the streets in the early 80's that could alter a person's mind for good. Or was I just loving the mask and not seeing the man behind the mask? There were times his eyes were glazed, and I knew he'd been drinking. But was he an alcoholic, a closet drinker, and I didn't see it? At times I would see him in a wooded area, watching me, and then he'd duck behind trees. At home when friends were visiting, I'd see him run into the garage and hide behind some junk and then sneak out, get into his truck and take off. At times, I would catch him leering at me with a strange look. What was going on with him I asked myself? This was not the man I thought I had married.

So I was on the loose, a woman scorned, and a woman free. He was living with her, and she was having his baby. It was time for me to move on. The court battle was like a black cloud hovering over me, as I wasn't truly free. I had to work so hard to make payments to lawyers and to maintain a house and a small acreage, some cattle, fifteen horses and a riding stable business. The first thing I did with my $10,000 inheritance was make a down payment on a tractor and loader so the work on the farm would be easier for me. To pay for the legal situation, I needed several other money-making activities. I struggled and didn't have time for a social life. But I still felt the urge to have someone love me and to love someone. This desire was stronger than anything else, and it made for many tear-filled, lonely nights.

Chapter 36: Honky Tonk Angels

From time to time, I could remember a song I heard about honky-tonk angels, it would play in my head quite often, after I had been in bars with my foster daughter, in order to take away my loneliness. This usually happened in summer, when tourists were in town. There were many men, mostly strangers.

The words came over the sound system and played into my heart as tears welled up in my eyes and took me back a few years. What was I doing in a bar trying to pick up this man, even if I felt single as my man was cheating on me and didn't want me? I should be at home in bed, next to my man, holding him. But he wouldn't be home; he was already sleeping with another woman. He would be somewhere, doing whatever men do when they're never home. So why did I feel guilty being in a bar? We were still married, and he was coming home the odd night. We weren't divorced yet, so there was always a chance he would change his mind. I just needed someone, a man in my life. I was tormented by these mixed feelings.

"Another round of drinks, bartender" a stranger at our table said. I did not say no. Maybe the drinks would make the pain go away, the ache that was so heavy in my heart. This man was interested in me; he wanted me, and I fell for his charm and the thought of the warmth of a body, any body, next to mine. I would not need to spend another night alone. I felt like a woman again, because for a short time I felt desired. It had been a long time since I'd felt that, and for a short time, the pain went away.

Why do men and women cheat on each other? Loneliness, pain and broken hearts? I questioned a few of the men about their wives going out and having fun. They couldn't understand why their wives were out drinking and flirting with men when they should be at home. So when this topic came up in our conversation, I asked them what they were doing at the pub, and their replies for the most part were pretty standard.

"Oh, we were just out with the boys for a few drinks, shooting a few games of pool, a bullshit session."

"Where was your wife when you left?"

"She was doing things around the house."

"Did you think of taking her out?"

"Oh, she wouldn't want to go anyhow. I deserved a night out after a hard week's work."

"Didn't she deserve a night out too?"

"I never thought about it that way."

"So what happened?" I asked with a smirk.

"Well, she showed up at the bar with a number of friends, drunker than a skunk, sexy clothes on, and flirting with all the guys. Made me sick!"

"And were you sitting with any women?"

"Well, a few women came to talk to us and sat down at our table." Typical scenario for disaster. The old double standard! Women left home alone when guys go out to "have fun with the boys" and try to act single. And with the drinks and feeling high, it's easy to get more involved with a woman sitting in a bar. There is her place or a hotel room after the bar closes. Why worry about this? It's only two drunks rolling around on a bed. It doesn't mean anything. I remembered those words from the past.

But it did mean something to me. It was humiliating and painful, and I had to face that woman, as she lived in my hometown! I knew that he slept with her, and I wondered how she could face me. Lonely women will do things when they can no longer stand sitting home alone, night after night, while their husbands go out with the boys and have what they call "fun" because they deserve it. There's always the game playing, the wanting to "get even" and show him that she can do this too. I was in that kind of mood off and on during those last five lonely years, I had while living with Brad.

Lonely women can become honky-tonk angels, as it says in the words of the song.

> ***What is love really? A rush to the brain, sex, co-dependency, comradeship? What does it really mean when someone tells you they love you?***

Back to the present. The word "love" is just a word. It can be a lie and it can mean nothing, just something said to get what a person wants out of another, make another feel good, or to make them feel good themselves. It's the action, or lack of action that truly shows love or lies, the little things one does for another, or the little things a person doesn't do. It's the heart beating rapidly, the happiness, contentment, and the joy of feeling loved. All of this is more than words; words can be fickle if they come from the mind. Words can be meaningless if they don't come from the heart.

Love comes from free will; it can never be forced. Even God has no control over free will. But it can be strong enough to move mountains, save a life, or take a life. Sex is the strongest attraction in the world, and love is the strongest emotion. Together they form a wholeness that can be the heaven on earth so many of us wish for and so few truly achieve.

Chapter 37: Upon Separation

I was a victim.

Denial is strong in both perpetrators and victims. Once I realized I had been a victim and was on the road to recovery, I was still blind to the amount of damage that had already been done to me mentally and physically.

After having a pillow placed on my head, my neck hurt for a long time. Migraines never ceased and post-traumatic stress sunk in years later, likely caused by the first discovery at the farmhouse. It took a while, but I was sure I had bounced back and life for me now would be normal, or as normal as possible after the deep scars were sealed up deep inside of me. I had a wonderful career, was good at whatever I attempted to do, and was still quite attractive and young looking and could be funny. People liked me, and men could fall in love with me. Once the court case was over, I could settle down to a life that would be good. The piece of clay I was could be molded into another shape and then hardened, to a rock. I loved my home, my place, my horses, my dog, my true friends, and my cats. I loved my town and the edge of the Canadian Shield where I lived. I loved my job; life would soon be good. One of the most eventful things I did, in summer of 1985, when Brad was no longer in my life, was to take a trip to the West Coast. I just jumped into my old car, and took off. On the way, I was amazed as to how free I felt. I could not believe what was happening to me. I felt like I was reverting back to the person I used to be, before the abuse started. I was me again and loved this feeling. A very huge load was lifted off my shoulders in spite of the legal issues hanging over me.

But my neck injury would never heal, and I became a victim to osteo-arthritis, which would hurt me for the rest of my life. And that day when a pillow was held over my face was the beginning of severe claustrophobia, in which I could not be in small places or have anything on my head, face and neck. In winter, I couldn't even wear a hood or toque.

The mental damage was subtle and deep, but it hurt me more than anything physically and was hard to get a handle on. What I didn't know then was that we are of a certain mold that attracts abusers or is it the other way around Are we attracted to abusers? Abusers have set patterns, and perhaps victims do as well.

I was victimized so easily and for so long because I had a mother who never showed me the love and approval I needed. She had her reasons, which were unknown to me at the time. Later I was told that she was very proud of me, and bragged about me to others, but she never told me this. I wish I had understood, but I didn't, because of the secrets my mother kept from me. I was needy for acceptance, for praise, for anything that would show her love for me, but I never got it from her. She was cold, in spite of the "dance" I did as a child to get her attention. There was never a woman role model in my childhood, other than her best friend, who showed me what little girls needed to do and know. I had no female to bond to, no sisters, no grandmothers and no mother. Perhaps that's why I stared at that picture of Minna Hitz, my maternal grandmother, so many times, wishing I could rub on it and she would appear magically to love me, hold me, and give me what I was so lacking as a teenager and an adult.

But I had a father and a wonderful brother who gave me what I was missing from my mother. They were the men in my life, so when I got to the age of marriage, it was men I turned to for what I was lacking. I trusted men because of the men I grew up with, who were honest, fair, and loving. I wanted to be spoiled, just like when I was a child, by a father figure. I didn't realize that not all men are capable of giving this kind of love to a woman, that there are many fakes and con artists that will promise the world and pretend to love, in order to get what they want. So I did the "dance" over and over, giving them everything I had, to earn their love for me. They took it and continued to pretend they loved me to keep me giving, and giving, and giving. I needed love, sex, and companionship, and when the man in my life was running around giving this to others, it hurt to the core of my being. My well was going very, very dry. I was getting thirstier and thirstier and more vulnerable. I would have fallen for any man at that time that could show me love or acceptance, things I didn't get at home, from my mother, while growing up.

Many of our problems in adult life originate in our childhood.

Because my father and I had looked after my mother from the time I was thirteen, I learned to become a care giver, and knew that there were people who needed looking after. Thus, I became co-dependent on someone needing my care. Perhaps that was the attraction. I needed to feel needed, and that translated to love as well. Would the man not love me if he needed me? To me this should be a given, yet I should have learned that there were people, like my mother, who were not capable of showing love, and that needing someone wasn't necessarily translatable to loving the caretaker. How twisted my childhood had made me! How ignorant I was of what love really meant. If I could only go back in time to fix things and make it right.

I also didn't realize that con men come in all colours and shades, all careers, all nationalities. They are so good at their deceitfulness, and they are the parasites who need the willing host. I was a willing host.

After going to EVOLVE in 1986, for ninety hours of group therapy, I deceived myself into thinking that never again would I fall for men like my husband. I knew it all now; I would not be as blind and would stay single for a while. I told myself that I needed no one. I could look after the riding stable myself, and I didn't need any man; I had a tractor that I had just bought. I was good to go ... alone! Superwoman was back again. EVOLVE gave me the education I needed, and now I felt that I knew it all. It was only later that I learned the most important lesson in life: the older you get, the less you know. Or is it the more you realize how much you do not know?

History is a series of chain reactions, of cause and effect. What happened to me in my first marriage and after would affect my next, and my next, and my next. How does one stop this chain? Good question! I wish I had at least thought about it and sought out some answers before feeling so smug about myself. A false sense of security gave me the illusion that I was okay. Superwoman was not okay and would not be okay for a long, long time.

Even though I was healing quickly, I still couldn't get vivid images out of my mind, from the cheating and the things he'd said. I wondered if they would haunt me for life. They did, and this was the beginning of post-traumatic stress, which had invisibly entered my subconscious mind, but wouldn't surface for many years when something triggered it, like shell shock for soldiers when they see something so horrific, it never leaves their heads. But it can be lived with, and may be less assertive in time, but this invisible guest never leaves us, just like thoughts of loved ones who leave this world remain with us for the rest of our lives. That's how grief works, and it applies to ex-husbands as well. We are needy for the attention, and after years of indoctrination, abuse is the attention, we feel we cannot live without. And when "honeymoons" are part of the abuse cycle, we often live for those beautiful moments, short as they may be.

I wished for a family, a sister, a mother, even a grandmother, someone to hug me in times of need. Someone to comfort me. There was no one, so I had to give myself the hugs I needed. I couldn't talk about my pain to my friends at the time I kept it inside of me, festering like a wound, poisoning me. I cried inside all the time but kept myself so busy I didn't feel it, while distracted. But things that festered, like a cancer, would grow and keep growing if not dealt with. Eventually it would eat away our soul, if we do not do something about it.

I looked at my grandmother's picture again after my mother passed away and wanted to know this elegant, stately woman. But I felt I never would, as there was no one left in my family on my mother's side to tell me about her. I thought that Minna went into the grave with my mother, as there seemed no way to look for her. How wrong I turned out to be! Minna was very much alive in her own way and would come back to caress me someday in a totally unimagined way!

Chapter 38: No One Told Me

In the back of my mind, I always resented the people who knew what Brad was really like and didn't tell me before I married him. Instead, they told me after we split up. Their reason was that I wouldn't have believed them. If they had told me, I would have had something to go by. I didn't have that *choice* as I had given Cindy, when I phoned her one day to let her know how Brad had treated me. She did not believe me. She had the choice and made it; she believed him and thought I was making things up. I did not have that choice! I didn't know the man or his background. I just knew the mask, and the mask looked good.

Why didn't people tell me? I wasn't sure I really wanted to marry him when he proposed, but he knew I wanted a ranch someday, and that was the drawing card, a dream of a ranch, as his father already had cattle and land, and he led me to believe some of these were his. I believed his lies and promises. It all seemed so perfect … too perfect to be real. I lived in an illusionary world, thinking he really loved me and we would have a family and a good life forever. Then I found out he'd said things to others like, "I won't have to work for a living now; when I marry her I will have my meal ticket" (meaning me, of course!). I learned he had always been a womanizer and manipulated people. It was a conspiracy if sorts, a conspiracy of silence. The relatives and friends knew him, but they didn't tell me about him. Drat, I might have not believed them, but at least I would have had choices and been able to think about it and see through his disguise. I would have become aware of the many signs. I was too blind until I saw it all for myself. I wasted so many good years of my life because of my lack of knowledge.

Had I known, I wouldn't have thought it was a mid-life crisis that he was going through, and I would have been more careful with my money, putting some aside for myself, for a rainy day. By paying all the bills, I fit into his plan. He had it all figured out, and his coming back to say he wanted to work things out was just a stalling technique to keep me paying all the debts and bills so he wouldn't have any but would still have time to dispose of assets and get money to pay for lawyers.

I was so blind and naive, but I would never be that way again. The heck with men! Just date them, have sex, and leave them, I thought. I didn't want to live with another man, as I'd been so burned by this one. Except, perhaps for Joe, if he were still available. Maybe he was the one I should have ended up with, or the man I met at Brandon College. I totally lost touch with that man, but I would see how Joe was doing. I phoned his parents' place in Saskatchewan after Brad told me to, in a taunting way. I needed to know why he'd dumped me in 1968. He was the only one who could tell me the truth, except for Brad, who never would. I phoned and asked where I might find him. I was in for the shock of my life. His father replied, "Didn't you know that he was killed in a helicopter crash in BC a few years ago?" I was absolutely stunned. He had married, and his child was born after he was killed. I would never get the answers I needed. Why had I waited for so long? Pride or what? Another big mistake in my life in not reaching out to people who had been reaching out to me all along, but I just ignored them. The life-long independent Superwoman!

It was hard living alone. Sometimes I needed a companion, sex, even a one-night stand. I guess when the well goes dry; one gets very, very thirsty! I'd lie on the couch and cry and cry, longing for companionship, love, anything. Even my ex would have been all right at that point. At least he'd be familiar, and there was comfort in that. My memories of sex with him were wonderful. Maybe I was associating sex with love, as it was love I so needed and I did not know the difference. It was later that I could understand a little of what I called the "fringe." Women living on the edge in small communities often were very promiscuous and the topic of coffee shop or hairdresser gossip. They were just lonely women with a low self-esteem who needed to feel wanted and figured that if a man wanted sex with them that was a sign of being wanted. Now I could see why I was so afraid of living alone.

Maybe I should go that way. At least I could find some relief. Hit the bars, let men take me home and screw me. Maybe that was what I needed. I was too busy teaching all day and working on the ranch at night to go places where I could meet nice man. How does one meet a man in a classroom, or on a trail ride, or maintaining my property? I had no life. I just had work, work, and more work, as I struggled to make ends meet, pay legal fees, and sort out the mess that my life had become. I did this for five years. I went to a few social events with girlfriends, where the object was a one-night stand to satisfy at least one of our needs, a quick fix. There was nothing serious, nothing in the love department, which was just an empty void. A very empty void. Not a life, just an existence! One day at a time, a passage through life with no joy, nothing to really to live for. A cold, empty void!

Chapter 39: A New Turn in My Life

One day a friend suggested a blind date with a man she was working for. Why not? It had been a long time since I'd gone on a real date. It sounded like fun. I went out with this man who seemed so sweet and affable, not particularly handsome, but had charisma. He could talk the talk, listened to me, was a gentleman, and said goodnight at the door without inviting himself in. It seemed too good to be true. I wasn't going to call him, because my self-esteem dictated that he wouldn't want me. I was no good. I needed proof to think he was interested, so he had to be the one phoning me. My ex-husband cheated on me constantly and told me many times that no man would ever want me, so I no longer felt worthy of being a wife, a companion, or a lover. Five long and lonely years reinforced this. Dating was a like a new game for me, and I no longer knew how to play it. I wasn't even sure I wanted to play it. There's a certain comfort when one gets used to living alone and establishes an independence that guarantees freedom from being hurt and abused! Freedom was power to me and gave me a reason to keep on living.

But *he* called me and, to my delight, asked me to go on another date. I was excited, and I wasn't going to miss out on it. It built up my self-esteem. He wanted to see me again and take me out, so I couldn't be all that bad. We dated for a while. At first we were friends but soon we became involved sexually, and that brought our relationship to a new level. He tried so hard to please me by saying all the right things. We talked about our past hurts and we listened to each other with compassion, providing support for each other's pain. He talked all the right talk and did the right things, and I thought, *Wow, maybe this is my future man; maybe this is the one I've been waiting for.*

We were moving too fast for my liking, but the thrill of "new" was there, and the hormones were talking louder than the brain.

A few months later he lost his job. He told me he was dying and that he missed his kids. What a witch, his ex-wife was, to take them away from him. All of this played on my heartstrings, and I wanted to help this man with his suffering, his obvious pain. After I got to hear his story, I fell, hook, line, and sinker for his lies. I was hungry for love and took the bait.

He wanted to move in with me after four months of dating and spending a lot of time together at his place or my place. He lost his job and so he offered to do things for me in the yard. He had a nice disability cheque coming "just around the corner," or so he said, and this would work for both of us. This sounded like a plan.

I should have said no, but I didn't.

Appendix

1. A Woman's Body found in Lac du Bonnet Residence May 6, 2009. When I spoke to her, earlier, she told me she had been abused and could not take it anymore. The RCMP first said the death was suspicious, but later determined it to be suicide.

2. "The Road Not Taken" by Robert Frost, 1874-1963, https.//poets.org/poet/Robert-Frost

   Two roads diverged in a yellow wood,
   And sorry I could not travel both
   And be one traveler, long I stood
   And looked down one as far as I could
   To where it bent in the undergrowth;. . .
   I shall be telling this with a sigh
   Somewhere ages and ages hence:
   Two roads diverged in a wood, and I—
   I took the one less traveled by,
   And that has made all the difference.

6. "Invictus" By William Ernest Henley, 1849–1903. https.//poets.org/poet/William-Henley

   Out of the night that covers me,
   Black as the pit from pole to pole
   I thank whatever gods there be
   For my unconquerable soul.

   In the fell clutch of circumstance
   I have not winced or cried aloud

Under the bludgeonings of chance
My head is bloody but unbowed

Beyond this place of wrath and tears
Looms but the Horror of the shade,
And yet the menace of the years
Finds and shall find me unafraid

It matters not how strait the gate
How charged with punishments, the scroll,
I am the master of my fate,
I am the captain of my soul.

7   Map of Prussia. My mother came from Marienwerder, in East Prussia and my father from the area of Konigsberg, a small hamlet of Memel. By original SVG file created by Matthead (based on East_Prussia_1939.kpg from English Wikipedia)

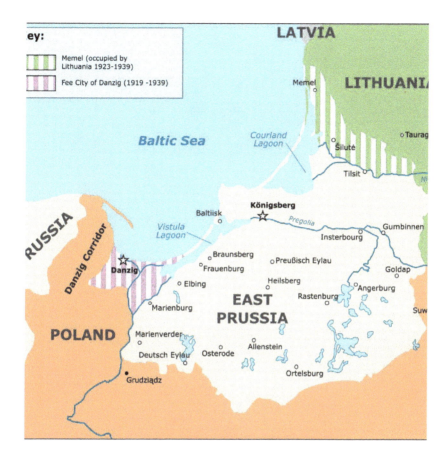

8 The Iron Cross 1914 was a medal ribbon (Eisernes Kreuz)

9 **Clay by White Wolf Woman**

Like a lump of clay,
I was molded into the shape
he wanted me to be.
I was soft and easily turned
into something I never was.
but now would be.
I no longer knew who I was,
only what he made me into.

His tools were words,
actions and gestures.
The result was not a form of beauty
but the form of a monster,
because he made me to be like him.

Then he left me
on the shelf to dry.
I dried out too quickly,
for a work of clay.
I crumbled and broke into pieces.
I shattered and became unrecognizable.
He tried to remold me.
Something strange happened; I suddenly
turned into a rock, as though I were
fired in a kiln.

The clay piece was no
longer pliable. It was solid
and that was when I knew that
I would not be moldable anymore
I had become a rock.

10 Three signs of abuse:

1. **Possessiveness.** Possessive of you as a person, your time, your friends, or anything he doesn't approve of. You are his possession, and no one else has the right to you.
2. **Control.** He controls everything you do. He will watch you, spy on you, chose who you talk to, and so on.
3. **Blame passing.** He will never take responsibility for any of his actions. Someone else is always as fault: he is never wrong.

[11] Post-Traumatic Stress Disorders, nimh.nih.gov/health/topics/post-traumatic-stress-disorder-ptsd/index/shtml

[13] The Abuse Cycle: The Honeymoon/Egg-Shell Walk/Blow

1. Honeymoon: flowers, gifts, passion, sex, charm, etc. This lasts as long as the nature of the cycle. It's different in different situations. A few days, a week, but not much longer.
2. Egg-Shell Walk: Things are starting to happen that make the victim wonder if the honeymoon is coming to an end. Little things, subtle things, like verbal shaming, picking an argument over nothing, complaining, saying hurtful things. This begins to escalate. The victim becomes anxious, as she always wishes to think that the honeymoon will last and things will be better. She realizes that maybe they won't get better but worse. She starts to anticipate the blow and is very careful not to upset the abuser, thus she walks on eggshells.
3. The Blow: It happens fast: a verbal barrage with profane language, threats, shaming, belittling comments, and then a storming out or going to bed alone, as though nothing has happened. Physical blows are much more pronounced than verbal blows but verbal abuse is hurtful, belittling, and demeaning. The perpetrator often leaves the house at this time to make the victim suffer more mentally, as she is alone and there is no making up at this point. If the abuser doesn't leave, the victim will, as she is afraid and seeks to escape. How could he, the man she loves and who says he loves her, do this to her?

Then back to the honeymoon. There is a lapse of time in which the abuser can think and starts feeling remorse. He brings flowers and gifts and says he is sorry. He promises he will never hurt her again. This can come in the form of a note, if the abuser is too ashamed to confront the one he hurts. This time is peaceful, so beautiful, like the sunshine after the storm, the heaven after hell. The victim lives for these times and thinks this is the time things will be different; things will get better but they never do. The abuser needs to seek professional help to readjust his attitude and reprogram his mind. Chances are slim that he will do it, until he sees consequences.

Some victims stay with the abuser for one of three reasons:

1. They are afraid to be alone.
2. They think they are to blame and if they learn to do things differently, the abuse will stop.
3. The blow is often the only attention the victim gets from the abuser. It almost becomes a sign of love to them. They become indoctrinated by the situation, like the Stockholm syndrome, and they bond even more with this intimate act that only they know about. They are also in denial and start to think that this is normal, as this is all they know.

[14] https://evolvecollege.ca/. Women's Evolve provides counselling to women who have experienced emotional, physical, or psychological abuse. They are located in Winnipeg, Manitoba, Canada and are a member of Klinik Community Health.

CPSIA information can be obtained
at www.ICGtesting.com
Printed in the USA
BVHW092006010821
613042BV00002B/8